KT-219-350

SALT-LICK RANGE

Salt-Lick Range

Lauran Paine

WHEELER
CHIVERS

This Large Print edition is published by Wheeler Publishing, Waterville, Maine, USA and by BBC Audiobooks Ltd, Bath, England.
Wheeler Publishing, a part of Gale, Cengage Learning.

Copyright © 1967 by Lauran Paine in the British Commonwealth.
Copyright © 2008 by Mona Paine.
The moral right of the author has been asserted.

ALL RIGHTS RESERVED

The text of this Large Print edition is unabridged.
Other aspects of the book may vary from the original edition.
Set in 16 pt. Plantin.
Printed on permanent paper.

LIBRARY OF CONGRESS CATALOGING-IN-PUBLICATION DATA

Paine, Lauran.
  Salt-Lick Range / by Lauran Paine. — Large print ed.
    p. cm. — (Wheeler Publishing large print western)
  Originally published: Bath : Gunsmoke, 1967.
  ISBN-13: 978-1-59722-974-6 (softcover : alk. paper)
  ISBN-10: 1-59722-974-1 (softcover : alk. paper)
  1. Large type books. I. Title.
  PS3566.A34S25 2009
  813'.54—dc22   2009002084

BRITISH LIBRARY CATALOGUING-IN-PUBLICATION DATA AVAILABLE

Published in 2009 in the U.S. by arrangement with Golden West Literary Agency.
Published in 2009 in the U.K. by arrangement with Golden West Literary Agency.

U.K. Hardcover: 978 1 408 44188 6 (Chivers Large Print)
U.K. Softcover: 978 1 408 44189 3 (Camden Large Print)

Devon Library Services

Printed in the United States of America
1 2 3 4 5 6 7 13 12 11 10 09

SALT-LICK RANGE

CHAPTER ONE

Judge Reginald Newcomb was a distinguished appearing man in his late fifties who sported a well-trimmed goatee and a splendid dragoon moustache. Even when people didn't have any idea what Judge Newcomb's qualifications for his exalted position were, he impressed them with his height, his frosty blue eyes, and his general appearance.

Judge Newcomb was a very able man. As an attorney, and later as Territorial Prosecuting Attorney, Reginald Newcomb proved himself capable over and over again. There was even some talk of electing him Territorial Governor of Idaho, but he was instead elevated to the rank of Territorial Superior Court Justice. It was in this capacity that Reginald Newcomb precipitated the Salt-Lick War.

Harper Todd down at Jefferson said Judge Newcomb should be tarred and feathered. Gray Appleby was for taking several thousand dollars from the war-chest of the Idaho Livestock Producers Association to hire a top gun with, and send him on up to Boise to assassinate Judge Newcomb.

Harper Todd was president of the Association, as it was called, and Gray Appleby was treasurer. They were both grizzled old cowmen worth a great deal in land and cattle, and other assets. Also, they both had title to land out on the salt flats east of Jefferson, where the trouble was centred.

Jefferson was a pleasant little cow town at the confluence of two clear-water creeks. It sat in an emerald valley with large cow outfits on all sides, except back towards the Roan Mountains, where the land was poor and gravelly and had at one time been brushed over with digger-pines and manzanita, but which had since been largely cleared by the settlers who'd begun arriving in the Jefferson country not more than five years earlier.

There was one other stretch of land the large cow outfits didn't inhabit: the Salt Lick. Up until the squatters started arriving, there had never been any need; all cowmen went out there with wagons and loaded up under a lemon-yellow sun, often visiting together out there on that baked white huge flat, sweating under the fierce brilliance, then creaking homeward with enough salt to keep their cattle supplied for months, and also with enough fresh gossip to keep the womenfolk titillated for an equal length of time.

Then the settlers also discovered the Salt Lick. Initially, as the petitions to Judge Newcomb had stated, the settlers had been content to do as the cowmen also did: load up a wagon or two, haul the salt home and store it for livestock and human consumption. That had lasted one year, the petitions said, then the settlers began going more and more often to the Salt Lick, quarrying greater and greater amounts of the salt, and finally they went whole-hog, sawing out big blocks, freighting them to rails-end and shipping them eastward to merchants who ground up the stuff and retailed it.

They made a huge hole out there. Cowmen couldn't any longer take along a cowboy or two, a sledge hammer and single-jack, and break off chunks of the salt. They had to take whole crews of men to get in and out of the quarry-holes, and on top of that invariably when they arrived out there, a mob of those settlers from the digger-pine foothills below town would be working like packrats, and the cowmen would have to establish a camp and sometimes wait several days to get to work.

Tempers simmered; the cowmen scorned the digger-pine people to begin with. They were down-at-the-heel squatters with rarely more than a team between two or three families of them. Also, although no one had proved it, cowmen had been losing a steer here, a cow there, since the advent of these people, and finally, they had pre-emptied the Salt Lick, which had heretofore always been exclusive cowman country.

There was a killing. It was inevitable. Or, as the U.S. Marshal for the Federal District of Western Idaho had written in his report, which had been included in the documents forwarded to Judge Newcomb, since no authority had been present, down there at Jefferson, to stop or even alleviate the snowballing rancour, it was only a matter of time before the factions clashed and someone was injured.

The "factions clashed" in mid June; one of the crew was under Harper Todd himself. The other crew was under Frank Talmadge, a slow-moving, slow-talking, tobacco-chewing Alabaman who did not appear to fear the Devil himself, and when Todd had told Talmadge to hurry it up and get out of the way so Todd's crew could get their loads of salt, the lanky and rawboned Alabaman had spat amber, gazed up at Todd on his saddlehorse and had said he and his neighbours would finish their quarrying in their own sweet time; if the cowmen didn't like that, why then they could go somewhere else and quarry.

Todd's rangeboss, Cleat Custis, called Frank Talmadge a fighting name, and when Talmadge went over and picked up his rifle off the seat of his wagon, Cleat Custis had shot and killed Talmadge.

Jefferson had been on a short fuse throughout the coroner's inquest, but nothing had happened. The main reason it hadn't was because the merchants of the town, who were strictly neutral, had formed a powerful vigilance committee, and had stood at the rear of the improvised courtroom with shotguns, and later, when folks filed back out into the beautiful summertime brilliance, the same vigilance committeemen were out there on the plankwalks, also with more shotguns. But the ill-will grew and intensified. When squatters or cowmen went out with their wagons and tools to quarry salt after that, they went in strength, and armed to the teeth.

As U.S. Marshal Fred Clampett said in his report, when he'd arrived in Jefferson, after hearing rumours of impending trouble out there, it was like riding into a community on the verge of open warfare. Todd's rangeboss had vanished. Todd had a new one; a quiet, long-limbed, hard-eyed man named Matt James. The U.S. Marshal caustically referred His Honour, Judge Newcomb, to the files in the Territorial U.S. Marshal's office up in Boise for further information relative to Matthew James. He also advised His Honour to look up the record of a man named Grat Younger, who had suddenly settled down upon a homestead in the digger-pine squatter community, south of Jefferson. Grat Younger had quietly ridden in and settled down one week after the killing of Frank Talmadge. That same week had seen Cleat Custis replaced as rangeboss for Harper Todd by Matt James.

For nearly a month after the killing of Frank Talmadge the squatters and cowmen backed and filled; when they met in town they were very careful to keep an eye on each other. When they met out at the Salt Lick, they stood off a fair distance and worked in shifts, one half of a crew quarrying while the other half lounged in a sentinel stance, with rifles and pistols.

Then Judge Newcomb made his decision: there was enough salt for everyone; the U.S.

Marshal would have a survey made dividing the salt flats; cowmen would quarry on one side of that line, the settlers would quarry on the other side.

If that seemed like a reasonable compromise to some, it certainly didn't seem like one to Harper Todd and Gray Appleby for the simple reason that between them they owned two sections of land running due north and south, or in other words, they owned two square miles which bisected the full width of the Salt Lick range, and Marshal Fred Clampett's survey, apparently ingnorant of this fact, drew the line of delineation for two miles from east to west. In other words, Clampett's dividing line put nearly a full mile of Todd's and Appleby's deeded land inside the area which the settlers could quarry.

The settlers knew this and loudly exulted over it, saying that the U.S. Marshal and His Honour up in Boise were on their side against the cattlemen. They strolled the roadway in Jefferson with taunting looks and broad smiles. They shifted most of their quarrying operation over onto the deeded land of Gray Appleby and Harper Todd, before Evelyn Benson told Marshal Clampett caustically at the Methodist Church Social, held annually on the first of July, that the one thing Jefferson had never needed was a stupid, ignorant, trouble-maker like — Fred Clampett. When he asked why she was so angry, Evelyn explained in precise and icy tones exactly what Marshal Clampett had done.

His reaction was chagrin. He went over to the court house, checked the records, discovered what a mistake he'd made, and re-called the Boise surveyors to read the riot-act to them about slipshod working methods. They were apologetic and offered to ride out with Marshal Clampett and make a new survey. This was done the first week in July when it was so insufferably hot out there on that baked white salt flat that the surveyor's chain-man had fainted. But Fred Clampett sat his horse as unrelenting as the Grim Reaper himself, and forced the Boise surveyor to finish his corrected line, which ran one mile further east of the old line to put the sections of deeded land inside that portion of the Salt Lick which the cowmen were to use.

While this was legally right, and also mor-ally right, when the squatters heard what had been done they turned on Fred Clam-pett like a pack of rabid wolves. But the U.S. Marshal hadn't really expected much else. What kept him in a black mood for several

14

days after the new survey markers were down, was the fact that the Boise surveyor had made the mistake, and had afterwards left Jefferson on the stage, leaving Fred Clampett back in Jefferson to shoulder all the blame.

Even the cowmen did not abate their resentment and rancour. Harper Todd said the Livestock Producers Association should hire an assassin — called "range detective" — and send him on up to Boise to sock away Judge Reginald Newcomb. Gray Appleby was in favour, but some of the less bold spirits in the Association demurred on the grounds that they had their Salt Lick back, or at least a big share of it, and while they thought that cussed judge up there in Boise ought to have his nose rubbed in it, having him killed was a little drastic.

No one knew what the settlers had to say; they were a secretive, closed-mouth bunch. Their initial wrath had been fierce and noticeable, all right, but after that they became quiet, and that, Fred Clampett told his superior up in Boise in a terse report, was in many ways much worse than a lot of gun wielding and shouts. The Territorial U.S. Marshal sent down Dan Miller, a youthful deputy, to work with Fred until the trouble atrophied, then Boise, with its

15

share of trouble elsewhere, turned its back in a figurative sense, on Jefferson, and Fred Clampett.

Dan Miller arrived in Jefferson on a pleasant July day, a little after high noon, wearing no badge and appearing no different from any other rangeman on the move. Even down at the liverybarn they scarcely gave Dan Miller a second glance. He was in some ways typical of the rangerider brotherhood. He was bronzed from exposure to the summer sunblast, his boots, hat, trousers and shirt were faded and worn, and his tied-down sixgun had the standard hard-rubber black grips put on every such weapon at the factory.

Dan was no more than twenty-five, perhaps an even six feet tall, carried no surplus weight, and had a pleasant, open countenance with friendly blue eyes. He was one of those thoroughly deceptive men who could have lived out his entire lifetime in some orderly eastern community without anyone ever even suspecting that he could and would, fight at the drop of a hat.

He didn't ask where the U.S. Marshal had his office. Instead, he strolled up through Jefferson until he saw the sign over a doorway mid-way between the liverybarn and the Great Northern Bar which stated the

16

Territorial U.S. Marshal for Western Idaho had his headquarters in that little slab building, then he went right on by up to the Great Northern for a drink of cool beer.

It was miserably hot out on the range, and even in Jefferson where there was some shade, the heat shimmered and bounced off tin roofs and glass windows. The Great Northern Bar did a land-office business in beer this time of year. Dan Miller had his share of it, too, that first day he arrived in Jefferson. He'd earned it; the ride down from the Snake River Valley was tedious, long, and uncomfortably hot.

CHAPTER TWO

Not very often, but occasionally Fate takes a hand in the devious affairs of men. Dan Miller ordered his beer from the barman at the Great Northern as innocent of troublesome intent as a man normally is in a place he's never visited before and among men who are total strangers.

Because it was breathlessly warm out the Great Northern had a fair-sized crowd, considering it was fairly early in the day. They were all rangemen; either riders or owners, but rangemen nonetheless, and they were enjoying their respite from the heat, the press of everyday obligations, and the sight of piney-woods settlers who were not welcome in the Great Northern Bar, which was an exclusive cowmen hang-out.

Then Deputy U.S. Marshal Dan Miller innocently observed to the barkeep that from what he'd seen of the countryside as he'd ridden in, perhaps someday the bar-

men wouldn't have to import their beer; that someday the folks would plant barley out there on the plains.

Perhaps under normal circumstances no one would have heeded that innocent remark, but these were not normal times in the Jefferson countryside; anyone talking of ploughing and sowing, regardless of his outward appearance, just had to be either another settler, or perhaps another hired gunfighter like Grat Younger, fresh-arrived in the country to make more trouble for the livestock producers. At least that was the barman's view of the remark, so he ambled around among his patrons repeating what Deputy U.S. Marshal Dan Miller had said, while Dan stood up there at the bar, one foot planted atop the brass rail, both elbows hooked over the rim of the bar, comfortably enjoying his cool drink, totally unaware that he'd kicked the lid off Pandora's Box until a heavy-boned, unshaven and battle-scarred cowboy heaved up to his feet from a poker game over across the room, hitched up his shell-belt and sauntered over to tap Dan on the shoulder. Dan turned — the burly man's heavy fist connected — and Dan went down with beer spilling over him, over the heavy-boned cowboy, and also over three or four impassive other cowboys standing along the bar nearby.

The rough-looking rangeman didn't say a word. He hardly even altered expression. For a moment he looked upon Dan with professional interest, perhaps a little surprised that Dan sat up blinking and shaking his head when any other man would have been totally unconscious after that unexpected blasting-hard blow, then he bent down to grab Dan's shirtfront and haul him up to his feet for the finishing blow.

That was a blunder. As the cowboy bent, Dan aimed his right hand and fired it. The blow caught the big man flush, staggering him. Before he caught his balance Dan was on his feet backing clear. By the time the cowboy shook out his cobwebs Dan was waiting for him, gently probing his jaw with one hand and gazing at the unshaven, thickly-made rangerider.

There wasn't a sound in the Great Northern Bar. All up and down the bar as well as out among the tables, men were intently watching. The barman was a stocky, short man, with arms like a blacksmith, a barrel chest, and a battered set of coarse features; he'd obviously weathered his share of storms like this one, and as he leaned upon his counter now, he was holding an ash wagon-spoke in his right fist. He clearly didn't believe he'd need to use the club, but was ready all the same just in case the bronzed, lanky stranger should, by some fluke, whip the rangerider.

It was very clear that none of the rangemen expected Dan Miller to triumph. When the unshaven man moved in, head tucked behind the curve of his left shoulder, right arm up, right fist cocked, the reason for this conviction was clear enough; Dan's adversary was an experienced battler.

But like nearly all snap-judgements, this one was also premature. Although Dan used no such professional crouch, his footwork was flawless and the lightning-like jabs and strikes he hit the heavier man with, showed that Dan Miller was no novice either.

The cowboy was trying to manoeuvre Dan up against the bar. Dan let him do that, almost, then he'd slide away. Once, the cowboy rushed him, exasperated at never getting quite close enough, and walked straight into a series of right and left crosses that stopped him cold, split his upper lip, knocked his hat across the room, and made him gasp from a belly-blow that forced him back. From then on, the big-boned man stayed away until he was ready, then jabbed. He tried next to keep Dan off balance and on the defensive, but that also failed. Dan was just too fast and too accurate.

Finally, the unshaven cowboy stepped back, dropped both arms and called Dan a fierce name, then said, "Fight, damn you! Stand an' fight!"

Dan did. He was out-weighed, so naturally everyone expected the sudden charge of the larger man to send him reeling, but the big cowboy's momentum pushed him straight-on into a rapier-like left hand which stung him, taking out some of his steam, then a sledging right hand came over, cracked across the bridge of the heavier man's nose, claret spewed, the cowboy's eyes helplessly rolled, and Dan stepped in to coldly and systematically cut him down. The final strike bent the cowboy over, retching. Dan stepped past, grabbed the man's shoulder, set himself and flung the cowboy over against the bar. He struck so hard three glasses on the back-bar shelf fell and broke, then he slid down into a rumpled heap.

For several seconds nothing happened. The barman hoisted himself up and leaned far over to peer downward. Dan reached, wrenched the ash spoke from the barman's right hand, tossed it into a corner and stepped back where his nearly empty glass of beer still stood. He was breathing hard, but more from excitement than from exhaustion. He raised the glass in his left hand and sipped, with his back to the bar, his right hand loosely hanging two inches above the butt of his sixgun. He gazed around where the customers were beginning to raise their eyes to him.

"Who's next?" he asked, drained his glass and set it to one side atop the bar.

No one was ready, right then, to accept his challenge. There were a dozen men in that room who'd choose Dan Miller with guns or knives or fists, but they hadn't quite recovered from the shock of seeing the man they'd evidently thought was invincible, cut down by a man an inch or two taller, but easily thirty pounds lighter. That would take a little getting used to.

Dan turned and beckoned the barman over. He mildly said, "A re-fill on that glass of beer, mister, and the next time you go for your wagon-spoke you're likely to lose it — and a couple of fingers along with it. Get the beer!"

The barman got it, set it down, stonily picked up the silver coin Dan put upon the bartop, and walked stiffly back down his bar. Like a lot of the other men in that quiet room, he evidently thought himself a rough-tough adversary, but also like the others, that recent and devastating upset he'd witnessed, shook both his confidence and his sense of how things should be. He wasn't going to brace Dan Miller.

From over near the door a lean, long-faced and pale-eyed man sitting sprawled behind a table with a bottle and one glass in front of him, said, "Stranger; 'you ever try buckin' a royal flush?" He didn't explain; he didn't have to. His left hand lay light atop his table, but his right hand was out of sight in his lap. He had a gun under there pointing straight over towards the bar.

Dan considered that man; he knew a professional when he saw one. He'd been a deputy U.S. marshal for five years, had tamed his share of frontier cow towns, and although the long-faced pale-eyed man's face was not familiar to him, he knew exactly what he was up against. And he did the only logical thing; in front of that roomful of witnesses, he deliberately turned his back on the pointed gun he couldn't see but knew was under there, lifted his glass of beer and sipped. The pale-eyed man wouldn't dare shoot him in the back. Not in front of fifteen or twenty witnesses, because no matter what the others thought of him, they wouldn't tolerate that kind of a murder. Back-shooting was the worst crime a man could commit in the cow country.

Then he said, "Put up the gun, mister, and either walk over here, or walk out of here into the roadway. I'll give you a better chance than you've got the guts to give me. An even break out in the centre of the road."

It was a fair offer. To every man in that room the challenge had been offered, and accepted. The rules were prescribed for this kind of a confrontation, too. Regardless of which man they wanted to see kill the other one, and there wasn't much doubt about that, the cowmen in the Great Northern were entirely in agreement with how the stranger was handling himself.

The pale-eyed man sat for a long moment gazing over at Dan Miller's back. The only sound was made when that broken and battered cowboy lying on the soiled floor against the bar, moaned in a bubbly way, and writhed a little. He was coming round, finally.

The pale-eyed man slowly holstered his gun, reached, poured himself a shot of whisky and said, almost casually, "Stranger; my name's Matt James. You remember that. I'm rangeboss for Harper Todd. That crack you made about puttin' in a big crop of barley don't go down well hereabouts — unless you're hirin' out to the digger-pine people over around Roan Mountain. In that case let me give you a little advice. Keep out of the Great Northern Bar. The settlers got their own saloons. We don't go into their bars an' we don't tolerate 'em comin' in here." Matt James threw back his head, dropped his liquor straight down and eased back in his chair again, slouched and relaxed, but keeping his humourless stare upon Dan Miller. "Now fish or cut bait; go join the digger-pine settlers, or stay here and be what you look like: a rangerider."

Dan turned slowly and set his back to the bar regarding Matt James. He knew the name, but this was the first time he'd crossed paths with the man who wore it. James was one of those shadowy men who never were actually beyond the law, although they teetered upon the razor's edge. He was a professional gunfighter, but as far as Dan knew, he'd never been an outlaw. There was a difference; sometimes it was so blurry and indistinct it scarcely existed, but it nevertheless was there.

"Pretty touchy aren't you?" Dan said. "I didn't claim I was going to plant any barley. In fact I wouldn't know how to go about it, mister. All I said was that someday. . . ."

"I know what you said," replied Matt James, reaching out for his bottle again. "But it was a poor thing to say in here, mister. This is cow country. It's goin' to stay cow country. You understand?"

Dan nodded, watched James down another straight shot, and turned back to finish his own beer. There was no point in pursuing that topic any further; they'd both said all that needed saying anyway. The barman walked over looking disgruntled.

"I got three broke glasses," he said, sounding truculent but only half looking that way as he regarded Dan. "Who pays for them?"

"How much, barkeep?"

"Two bits."

Dan put down a quarter of a dollar and pushed it over. He thought a moment, looked down where the heavy-boned and unshaven cowboy was pushing himself up into a sitting position, dropped another two-bit piece beside the other one and said, "Give ol' rough-'n-tumble here a stiff shot, barkeep. He sure-Lord needs it."

Then Dan finished his beer, and walked almost out of the saloon. At the door a blue-eyed tough-faced man wearing a badge appeared, blocking Dan's exit. He was impassive and made no move to step aside as he ran a slow gaze around the room, then held out his left hand.

"Your gun, stranger," he said softly. "We'll talk it over down at the jailhouse whether

27

you get it back or not."

Dan offered no argument, no resistance, he handed over the gun, walked on outside and paused out there looking at the men standing back, wondering which one of them had run for the U.S. Marshal. It could've been any of them. He stepped down into the roadway and went plodding along in the general direction of the marshal's office, which was a log and mud building with walls three feet thick, and which had two large steel cells out behind the office, like the cages wild animals were kept in.

People gawked; mostly, they didn't know what all this was about. They'd eventually hear, of course, but right then they stopped and turned to watch Fred Clampett take his prisoner on down to his office, and inside.

As soon as Fred had the roadside door closed, he blew out a big breath and shook his head. "I like your entrances," he sardonically told Dan Miller. "The last time we worked together over at Palouse, you managed to shoot off your mouth in the blacksmith shop."

Miller grinned. "Yeah; well it was wintertime then, Fred, an' all I was tryin' to do was get warm. This time it's hotter'n the hubs of hell, and all I wanted was a cool drink of decent beer."

"Did you get it?" Marshal Clampett asked, with deceptive mildness, as he tossed Dan back his sixgun.

"Yeah. It was pretty fair beer too. But all I said up there was that if someone'd plant barley around here, folks could make their own beer."

Fred dropped down at his desk. "I see," he said, swinging around in his chair to gaze at the younger man. "True to form, Dan, you're still makin' a habit of saying the wrong thing at the right time. Well; maybe just this once you accidentally did us both a favour."

"How?"

"Matt James and his friends up there think you're maybe a hired gun for the settlers. If we're smart maybe we can just use that somehow, because the one thing we really need to prevent trouble here, is information. I feel like a leper; no one talks to me if they can possibly avoid it, and when they do talk to me, they only discuss the weather. But all the same, there's trouble comin', Dan, and you're goin' to be square in the middle of it."

CHAPTER THREE

The weather continued hot. For Dan Miller it continued hot in more ways than one. He'd been in the Jefferson City area four days and except for some hard looks from an occasional rangerider he crossed trails with out on the range, he met with about as much of a welcome as a scorpion might have expected.

He got to know Roan Mountain, the digger-pine homesteads over around there, the back trails and the roadways, all by sitting upon a shady ledge half way up Roan Mountain where trees grew and grass was adequate for his horse.

He also got to know the cattle outfits the same way; not by invitation, but by observation while he skirted out and around. It was a satisfactory way of becoming oriented in strange country, but also, it was the lonely way.

Lonely, that is, until the fragrant early

morning with brilliant sunlight all around that he rode around a large old grey-rock headland after breaking his camp near a sweet-water spring, and came face to face with three unpleasant-looking individuals sitting their horses as though carved from stone, who had evidently been waiting for Dan.

He started to raise a hand in greeting and the foremost man over there lifted his fist over the saddle-swells; he had a cocked forty-five in it. Dan recognized that man: Matt James. He thought the other two men had also been at the Great Northern the day of his fight there, too, but he wasn't sure of that at all.

"Shuck your gun," James ordered.

Dan considered the unsmiling threesome. "What for?" he asked.

James explained. "Because you're goin' with us to pay a visit to a feller named Harper Todd, an' if you're unarmed it'll be a lot easier all around."

Dan plucked out his sixgun, twisted in his saddle, dropped the weapon into one of his saddlebags and straightened forward again "Satisfied?" he asked. James nodded; he was satisfied.

"Now turn around, cowboy, and ride northeast. We'll be on both sides an' in

31

back. You savvy?"

"I savvy," said Dan, and let them herd him along. He knew where he was going anyway. He'd picked out the Todd outfit first off because of what Marshal Clampett had told him about its owner. He offered to make conversation twice, on the way to the ranch headquarters, and both times he was silently rebuffed, so, as they entered the yard and crossed towards a huge log barn where several men were idly standing and talking, he turned quiet and watchful.

Harper Todd's ranch was large and obviously prosperous. Todd himself, grizzled, uncompromising, and hard as iron at fifty years of age or thereabouts, watched his men bring Dan Miller over to him in front of the barn. Todd neither moved nor altered expression as the riders halted across the hitchrack from him.

One of the men standing there with Harper Todd was Gray Appleby; Dan had familiarized himself with the Appleby outfit too. It lay northeast of Jefferson, which actually was well out of the range of the ranches which bordered Roan Mountain's unfenced cow range. And Gray Appleby, a few years younger than Harper Todd as well as being several inches shorter, also kept six rangeriders and one rangeboss. Between them, those two men standing there controlled fourteen rawhide-tough riders; they were, Dan knew, the men who would call the shots if trouble came; aside from being the biggest cowmen and having between them the greatest number of rangeriders, they were also the most influential members of the Association.

"Here he is," said Matt James to Harper Todd. "He was camped on our range last night, southwest, down by the granite point."

Todd considered Dan for a moment. He and Appleby were hard-eyed and obviously confident. The men standing around and behind them looked the same way; they clearly were other members of the Association, and to Dan this looked like some kind of pre-arranged unofficial Association meeting.

Todd said, "All right, Matt; that's all for now." He waited until James and his two companions turned and jogged back out of the yard before he said, "Miller; you've been seen a lot lately, ridin' here an' there, lookin' things over, sizin' up the ranches an' the cow-crews. These men with me this mornin' are members of our local cowmens' association. They've been gettin' reports from their riders about you. Not just in town, but on the range as well. I'm tellin' you this because I like all the cards on the table when there's a showdown. It sort of clears the air; everybody knows where we all stand."

Dan nodded. This was candid talk. It inspired respect. If Todd didn't ruin it all now by turning out to be underhanded and deceitful, things might not turn out to be as bad as Fred Clampett was certain they were going to turn out.

Todd went on speaking, standing easy over there and keeping his hard, knowledgeable eyes upon Dan Miller. "What we want a frank answer about, Miller is this: Are you spyin' for the digger-pine men, or aren't you working for them?"

Dan could answer that very simply, but the trouble was, that as soon as he did so, then Todd's next question was going to be more direct and personal: Who was Dan and what was his business in the Jefferson country, and by mutual agreement with Fred Clampett, Dan couldn't answer that because he and Marshal Clampett had decided, at least for the time being, it would be better if no one knew Dan was a deputy U.S. lawman.

The cowmen standing there along the front of Harper Todd's big log barn waited. They, like Todd himself, did not like Dan's delay in answering; it showed on their faces. Dan leaned upon his saddlehorn, gazed at them all, then concentrated upon Todd himself as he said, "I don't work for you, and I don't work for the settlers, but I like the country, so I figured, if I aim to stay hereabouts, what with trouble in the making and all, it'd be wise to get to know the outfits an' the lay of the land, first. And if I'd been spyin' on anybody, Mister Todd, believe me, you wouldn't have known it if I hadn't wanted you to."

"You are for hire?" Gray Appleby asked. "That feller you whipped in the saloon in Jefferson rode for me for two years. Yesterday he quit and rode away. I need a replacement for him."

Dan caught the innuendo there; Appleby was implying that Dan owed him something for causing one of his riders to quit. He said, "I'll let you know, Mister Appleby," and twisted in the saddle to dig out his sixgun and drop it back into his hip-holster. Then he said, "Mister Todd; this here makes the second time your rangeboss's got the drop on me. The next time it's not goin' to work out the same." He lifted his reins and Todd scowled.

"Hold it, cowboy. You just gave me a warning. Now I'll give you one. Don't line up with the settlers. If you do you'll be linin' up with the losin' side. We won't bother you any more. Not until you make up your mind who you're going to ride for. Then you'll either have a small army of good friends, or good enemies. Think it over.

Dan nodded, turned and walked his horse out of the yard. He saw two horsemen, one to the north, one to the south, sitting their saddles a half mile out, watching which way he rode. One of those men was Matt James, he'd have bet good money. It crossed his mind that he and James were riding a collision course.

He let his horse pick its own route and gait, knowing he was being watched. The animal struck out for the same place Miller had camped the night before. The grass and water were excellent over there. To the horse as well as the man, trouble seemed very distant; little more than a small dark cloud far off on an otherwise golden horizon.

Fred Clampett had been firm on the point that trouble was imminent and inevitable. To lanky Dan Miller, riding over the warming land in the summertime morning, it seemed so distant he scarcely considered it at all. But Dan Miller didn't know this land as well as Marshal Clampett did; neither did he know its people.

36

He off-saddled out where he'd had his nighttime camp, hobbled his animal and went back to dump his gear in the trampled grass again. He had a whole afternoon to kill, and Dan Miller knew the art of loafing. He also knew he was being watched, and that half-annoyed, half-amused him.

Where his grey-rock headland lay was along the southern border between cowmen and digger-pine men, but so far at least he'd had no brush with the settlers. As the afternoon progressed, though, that changed. Four riders came down off the slopes of Roan Mountain in reply to a dazzling heliograph signal southward around the grey-rock headland where Dan couldn't see it, and made their deliberate way on across the range directly towards his camp.

When they approached out in plain sight making a point of letting him see them long before they got close, he had plenty of time to assess their looks and guess their probable purpose. By the time they solemnly rode into his camp, nodded and dismounted, he had his answers ready. He also had just begun to wonder if perhaps he hadn't been wrong and Fred Clampett hadn't been right, for those settlers were evidently full of the same curiosity about Dan Miller as the cattlemen had also been.

He knew which one was Grat Younger. He also knew two of the other slab-sided, hard-eyed men with Younger. They had their stump-ranches over against the mountain. They were sly-eyed, raffish men who made no pretence at being anything other than what they were; they didn't dress nor act like cattlemen. Also, they didn't much favour the stubby-barrelled Winchester carbines rangemen carried, but seemed to prefer the longer barrelled rifles of other parts of the country.

Younger was a dark-eyed, dark-haired man, stringy and sinewy in build. He dismounted and stood with one hand still draped around his saddlehorn, quietly eyeing Dan Miller, while the men with him, all three of them, made a point of staying a step or two farther back. It was obvious to Dan Miller that when Grat Younger rode out, he was boss. Those settlers looked around as though to be certain they were alone with Dan in this place, then gradually relaxed, waiting for Grat Younger to speak his piece.

Grat was in no hurry. He was a Missourian with that peculiarly sectional droopy-eyed look, and the manner, Missourians often had. When he'd completed his long study of Dan, his horse, his saddle and guns and bedroll, he was ready to talk.

"Mister," he said, "seems to us settlers you been downright interested in what we been doin', and where we live, an' all. So we'd sort of like to know a little about you, too."

Dan waved his arm. "Fair enough," he said. "Sit down, fellers." No one sat; no one even moved. Grat Younger stood exactly as he'd been standing; one arm carelessly flung around his saddlehorn, his body loose and hip-shot beside his horse.

Dan shrugged as though to tell the digger-pine men to suit themselves about whether they sat or not, and said, "Sort of half a no-tion to settle hereabouts. I like the country, so I been gettin' acquainted with it. There's talk of trouble over at Jefferson, an' that makes a man sort of careful. I've been makin' a point of findin' out where would be the best place for a man to stand, to keep clear of it. And mister, that's about the size of it."

Grat Younger didn't move. He studied Dan's features a while before he said, "Mister; if you're not a spy for the cowmen's association, then you probably been a cowboy. At least you look the part of one or the other, an' from this big rock south an' west is settler-country. You go to ridin' up on Roan Mountain any more, a-settin' an' a-watchin', an' you're goin' to get killed. Seems to me that's right simple to understand. How does it seem to you?"

"Right simple to understand." spoke up Dan Miller promptly. "Right simple. But if I'd been hostile, mister, I'd have done my meanness by now — an' since none's been done, you ought to see I'm not sidin' with anyone."

Younger's companions looked at him. He finally moved; heaved himself upright off his horse and dug around in a pocket, drew something forth and tossed it down in the dust over where Dan Miller was sitting. It was a flattened bullet.

"I'm not right sure that ain't your'n," Younger said. "So maybe you did your meanness already — and missed. But mister, the next time you shoot at one of the settlers like was done this morning — either miss a full mile or don't miss a fraction of an inch — because I'll be comin' for you if the next one lives to tell about it."

Dan picked up the flattened slug, hefted it, gazed at it, then raised a perplexed look to Grat Younger. Obviously, Younger did not believe Dan had fired this bullet, otherwise he wouldn't be standing there looking so calm about it.

"Mister," Dan said. "If you mean I bush-whacked someone this morning you're dead wrong an' I can prove it."

Younger nodded. "Yeah; we got our own ways of knowin' things too, stranger. You were hauled over to the Todd place this morning an' been over there right up until a while ago. But my point is, stranger: Be almighty careful. Maybe you got a pardner who done that bushwhackin' this morning. Maybe you don't know anything about it. Until we know one way or another, stranger, just be damned careful, 'cause whether you know it or not, you been ridin' the edge of the blade for the past few days." Younger turned, stepped up over leather and settled himself as he evened up his reins and said, "One more thing, stranger: If you're really not with the Association, an' need a livin' wage with grub thrown in, ride on into Jefferson and tell the nighthawk at the liverybarn. He'll send us word."

Younger turned and rode off. The other three settlers jogged stiffly along behind him. Dan sat there gazing after them for a while, then turned back to hefting that flattened lead bullet in his palm. He'd been appraised by both factions now, and had been offered employment by both. Of course he couldn't accept either offer, but it struck

41

him that Fred Clampett was right, after all, and he was wrong; trouble *was* coming. In fact it was very near, otherwise the divergent factions wouldn't be out recruiting.

He considered the sun, went after his horse, saddled up and rode eastward. The plan had been for him to meet Fred Clampett at the grey-rock headland, but obviously this was out of the question. He was under surveillance by the cattlemen and digger-pine men both. If he stalled until nightfall he'd probably be able to see Fred without being caught at it. If they saw him with the U.S. Marshal, they'd have all the answers both sides needed, and while right now both sides viewed him with scepticism, they nevertheless were willing to let him make his choice. The other way, they'd both raise their sights a notch for him. They might both be ready to fight one another, but there was one foeman they both seemed dead-set against — U.S. Marshal Fred Clampett.

Dan rode. He made a big sashay over Todd's range as though bound for the country over east of town, most of which belonged to Gray Appleby. To any watchers he looked to have a definite destination because he rode deliberately and consistently, but as shadows lengthened, he slowed

42

until his horse was just poking along. At the same time he kept a close watch southward along the edge of Jefferson where Clampett would ride out. He was praying it would be fully dark by then, and since he'd had all the bad breaks a man needed for one day, he was now entitled to a good break, and he got it.

Marshal Clampett left town in a steady walk, riding west, just before the sun completely dropped away. Dan recognized him, let the darkness fully settle, then swung his mount and went down to intercept Clampett and draw him away from where they were to rendezvous.

CHAPTER FOUR

They rode southward three miles to a rendezvous-spot Marshal Clampett knew of. It turned out to be a rocky place where in years past the two white-water creeks which skirted the town and came together down-country, had savagely flooded over several acres sweeping away all earth and leaving behind only a large jumble of big boulders and rocks. No one ever visited this place, Marshal Clampett said, dismounting under the cobalt heavens and picking his way over where a few low, smooth stones formed passable seats.

Dan told him what had happened with Matt James and Grat Younger. Clampett didn't appear surprised. About that bushwhacking, he said he'd already been informed of it by the settlers, and while it didn't mean a whole lot, since the bushwhacker had missed, it nevertheless proved his point: Settlers and cattlemen were getting rigged out for serious trouble.

"One of the settlers was out with his team working a field. When he passed near a stand of digger-pines, someone tried a long-range shot at him. The slug struck a wagon wheel." Fred shrugged. "That's all there was to it."

Dan fished out the slug Grat Younger had tossed at him. "Not quite," he said, and removed a carbine bullet from his shell-belt, pried out the lead and held those two slugs out. "Take one in each hand," he told Fred Clampett, and when the marshal had complied, Dan said, "Notice anything?"

Clampett nodded and peered closely at the bullets. "The flattened one is heavier."

Dan said, "When Younger tossed me the thing I noticed that, too. Fred; that's not from a carbine, that flat slug's from a rifle."

Clampett looked up, his gaze level and steady. "This is interesting," he murmured. "Now why would one of the digger-pine men take a shot at another digger-pine man?" Fred leaned back upon his rock, dropped both slugs into a vest pocket and scratched his head. Dan sat there fashioning a smoke, saying nothing. He'd long since come to his own conclusion on this score. Now he waited for Fred Clampett to arrive at his conclusion. He lit up, inhaled, exhaled, and softly smiled.

Clampett said, "All right; I know what you're thinkin' — that whoever shot at the sod-buster was another sod-buster, not a cowman at all, because the rangemen don't carry those lighter carbines. You figure someone over there in the Roan Mountain community's tryin' to edge the trouble over the salt lick into a real war. All right, Dan — who?"

Dan flicked ash and looked at the senior law officer. "You know 'em better'n I do," he answered. "Not only who — but why?"

"I just said — to stir up the trouble and bring it on to a shootin' scrap."

"I didn't mean that when I asked why," Miller retorted. "I meant *why* does he want the trouble to start; what axe has he got to grind?"

Fred Clampett fished out his own makings and dropped his head thoughtfully while he too made a cigarette, and afterwards he said, with smoke trickling from both nostrils, "Grat Younger? Maybe to keep the payments comin' in from the digger-pine men. 'Sound reasonable?"

Dan said that it sounded reasonable. He then said he thought Fred should ride out and have a talk with a few of the digger-pine men around Roan Mountain; piece together as much information as he could.

Fred agreed to that, then he too had a suggestion. "Stay off the range for a day or two. Hang around town. If both sides are keepin' an eye on you it'd be better not to let either one get any ideas that you're helpin' the other faction. After all, what I want to do is *prevent* trouble, not cause it by getting you shot."

Dan stood up. "That's right neighbourly of you," he drily said. "Now that you mention it, I'd as soon no one shot me, too." He killed his smoke, twisted to look all around, and to listen a moment, then as he faced forward again he said, "Marshal; it's beginnin' to look to me like their salt trouble is only part of it."

Fred had an answer for that. "Any time men get in a fightin' mood, they don't much care what their initial reason for fightin' was; their attitudes change and all they want is blood. It's the same here, or in a big war. The *will* to fight is what drives folks, once they get their dander up. The salt started it; when a feller named Frank Talmadge got killed, that cinched it. The digger-pine folks have always felt the cattlemen are too rich an' powerful and well-established. But now they've got their martyr as well as their hired killer — Grat Younger — so they're ready to

47

go. Maybe if the cowmen had also lost a man it wouldn't be so bad, Dan, but that hasn't happened, so they got a reason to want vengeance. At least that's how I see things. That's why I told you trouble was coming."

"And suppose they pick off a cowman, or some rangerider," said Miller. "That might satisfy the digger-pine ranchers, but all it'll do for the cowmen is set them nightridin' with guns and torches. So, you're goin' to lose either way, Marshal. If they kill a cowman, the ranchers'll hit back hard. If nothing happens to soften up the digger-pine folks, they'll still be plottin' their vengeance for this Talmadge feller. Nice kettle of fish you have."

"Glad you like it," mumbled the senior peace officer, arising and dusting his britches. "Because you're goin' to be smackdab in the middle of it."

They traded a look, Clampett offering a little humourless grin and Dan Miller looking back the same way, then they parted, each heading for town, but by different routes, and later, when Dan rode into the liverybarn he saw the marshal's horse already stalled and eating. He also took a long, hard look at the nighthawk, who was a thick-necked, paunchy individual with tight

48

curls of wiry hair atop a bullet-head. It occured to Miller as he handed his animal over to this man, that he'd neglected to tell the marshal who the digger-pine-settlers' spy in town was. But as he sauntered out into the pleasant, star-lit night, he thought it very probable that Clampett already knew that anyway, and set his steps in the direction of the Great Northern Bar.

He hadn't progressed ten feet from the roadway doors through tobacco smoke thick enough to be cut with a knife, before he saw Matt James and the pair of buckaroos who'd been with Matt that morning when they'd disarmed Dan and driven him to the Todd place. They also saw Dan, over their shoulders in the back-bar mirror, but none of them so much as turned his head.

The room was large and dark except for the overhead kerosene lanterns with their glaring reflectors. It was also crowded and noisy. Several card games were in progress, the bar was well lined, and elsewhere men stood and talked, or sat with private bottle and seriously drank.

Dan went around where the bar turned in towards the wall, nodded at the night barman and waited. No one was particularly heeding him, although now and then he caught a rider gazing his way. Evidently most of them knew who he was. His drink came, he flipped down a coin and hooked the glass to him with his left hand. On each side of him were other solitary drinkers; they were looking stonily straight ahead, completely occupied with their drinking.

Matt James turned, eventually, face red, eyes very bright. Dan saw the look and his heart sank. He wasn't afraid of James, he just didn't want any more trouble. He tried looking elsewhere, but James stepped back and turned. Dan sighed with resignation, finished his whisky and waited. James came around the bar, halted and said, "Hey, grub-liner, how'd you make out with ol' Todd this morning?"

"Fine," said Dan keeping his voice down and mightily hoping Matt James would do the same.

But James had a load on; at best he was taciturn and surly and very confident. Drunk, he was unpredictable to Dan Miller, but dangerous, so Dan turned a little and watched him.

James said, "I got that message you sent me, about gettin' the drop on you twice, but not again."

" 'That so," mumbled Dan. "Care for a drink?"

"Nope. 'You tryin' to talk yourself out of

somethin'?"

"Maybe," Dan candidly retorted. "There's a time an' a place for everything. Tonight's neither one. I'm in here for a nightcap. That's all."

"Well, well," murmured Matt James, making an incorrect syllepsis. "Got you a little worried, eh, grub-liner?"

"Have a drink," said Dan, feeling the eyes of the men on each side of him coming to bear upon him.

"I don't need a drink, grub-liner. I need a fight."

Dan looked along the bar. Matt's two rangeriding friends were watching, wide grins across their faces. The two men on each side of Dan, though, weren't grinning; they were gazing upon Dan with disgust.

Dan shook his head at James. "You don't need a fight," he said. "You're drunk, James."

The long-faced gunfighter quirked his thin lips into a grin. "You just insulted me," he said. "That's all the reason I need."

On both sides of Dan the men pushed back, getting clear. Elsewhere, though, the width and breadth of the saloon, no one appeared to realize what was happening down the bar, in next to the wall. The noise and movement continued unabated. Even the night barman, who, like all vocational barkeepers ordinarily had a nose for smelling out impending trouble so it could be quelled swiftly with a wagon-spoke, entirely missed out.

"Let's see whether I can get the drop a third time," said James, standing loose and ready, still sardonically grinning.

Dan turned as though to put his back to James as he'd done once before, but this time it was a ruse. He thought he knew what James would do, and Matt did it; he lost his hard smile, uttered a growl and stepped forward to catch Dan by the shoulder and wrench him around off the bar.

James still had his left arm high and fully extended to grab hold, when Dan whirled and struck. Matt James took that blow up alongside the head near the temple. His eyes floated upwards, his arm dropped down, and his gun-hand turned as limp as putty. Then he simply folded forward at the knees and fell into the bar.

Dan caught him, eased him gently down into a sitting position, and dropped his right hand straight down as those two smiling rangemen down the bar who'd been drinking with Matt James, looked both petrified and astonished.

The barman came walking on up. Dan

could see all along the bar from where he stood around the corner and in next to the wall. As the barman flicked his hand under, reaching for his ash billet, he and Dan were looking straight at one another. Dan gently shook his head. For a couple of seconds the barman still reached, but when his thick fingers came into contact with the spoke, they didn't close around it. The man straightened up, uncertain and careful.

Men no more than ten feet away who'd been looking in other directions and hadn't seen Dan crack Matt James alongside the head, still had no idea violence had erupted.

Those two rangeriders pushed off and came walking around to stop and stare down. James was slumped and out cold. Dan kept an eye on those two as well as upon the bartender.

One of the cowboys said, "Hell; he was drunk. All you had to do was push him off balance."

Dan made a little face about that. Drunk or stone sober, Matt James'd had his right hand within a fraction of an inch of drawing his forty-five. No one, least of all a professional peace officer whose trade for the past five years had been dealing exclusively with men like Matt James, would make the mistake, or take the chance, of trying to push Matt James off balance.

"Take him out into the fresh air," said Dan. "And don't get heroic, either one of you."

One of those cowboys bent to grasp the unconscious man's shirt and haul him upright. The other one took Dan's measure with a slow, careful stare, then he said, "Mister; you been awful lucky this past week, traipsin' around where you had no business. But a couple minutes back you tore it for good an' all. If you're still around Jefferson when Matt sleeps this one off tomorrow, he'll come huntin' you. An' Matt James don't miss!"

"Thanks," said Dan, "for the warning. Now give your pardner a hand and haul him out of here."

Finally, men sat up and looked. Matt James being lugged out of the Great Northern feet first, was something to be surprised about, evidently.

CHAPTER FIVE

Evelyn Benson was five feet and four inches tall. She was twenty-one years old with black hair and creamy-golden flesh. She worked at the *Jefferson General Store* as a combination clerk and bookkeeper. And also, she had dark grey eyes which sometimes, when the occasion arose, became nearly as black as her hair.

She was solidly put together; when Evelyn Benson walked there wasn't a wiggle anywhere, nor a jiggle. She was a large-breasted, deep-hipped girl, with muscle. She was also very handsome, with a heavy mouth, a nose that tipped up just the smallest bit, and black brows above her gun-metal eyes.

When Dan Miller sauntered into the general store for a box of .45 bullets the morning after his brush with Matt James, he no more expected to see anything like Evelyn Benson in Jefferson, let alone in the general store, than he expected to reencounter Matt James. She came along to get him his bullets because the only other clerk — an elderly man — was already busy with other customers.

Dan stared. Evelyn's grey gaze began to darken slightly, but she didn't drop her eyes as she put down his box of shells and told him the price. He dug for the money. They each took the measure of the other, then Evelyn bluntly said, "Do you really think it's worth it, Mister Miller, strutting around town to make a big impression, before Harper Todd's men get here and kill you?"

Dan put the money down and raised his eyes. "I've just seen the only reason," he said right back, "in this whole lousy countryside — not just the town — why I'd stay here one minute longer."

She didn't blush. She didn't drop her eyes nor change the subject, nor do any of the little weakling things women usually do when a man turns bold towards them. She simply said, "They'll kill you before high noon. Unless of course you saddle up and ride over to Roan Mountain. Or unless you just keep on riding and never come back."

"Ma'am," Dan said. "Do you mind telling me your name?"

"It's Evelyn Benson. My uncle and aunt own this store. I clerk here for them. I was

56

born in Missouri, I'm twenty-one years old, and for the good it'll do you, I've yet to see a man in Jefferson worth looking twice at."

"You're plumb right," conceded Dan, picking up his box of shells. "I haven't either." He gave her his most disarming smile. "I'm interested, ma'am; how did you know my name?"

She was ironic towards him. "Why Mister Miller; nearly everyone knows who you are by now. You're the man who whipped Gray Appleby's wrangler, and who last night knocked out Matt James. Believe me, Mister Miller, the folks of Jefferson know exactly who you are." She scooped up the money for the shells he'd put down, and as she turned away she said, "The undertaker particularly knows who you are!"

Dan went back outside. It was still quite early. He saw Marshal Clampett leaving town down at the liverybarn, heading in the direction of Roan Mountain. He also saw that paunchy, bull-necked hostler down there watching Clampett ride off. That was the man who was spying for the settlers, that kinky-haired liverybarn dayman.

For lack of anything better to do, Dan sauntered down by the telegraph office, stepped up into a recessed doorway, made a smoke and watched the hostler. It proved an enlightening long moment. When the liveryman had a free moment he climbed into the loft, and moments later Dan saw the quick, dazzling flash of heliograph light. He couldn't actually see the hostler standing up there in the loft doorway facing west, making those signals, because he was around front and across the road, but he knew the flash of sunlight off polished steel or glass when he saw it.

He blew out a big bluish cloud thinking that those digger-pine people would know Marshal Clampett was coming for two hours before he even got close. He also thought those settlers out there weren't likely to be caught off guard. If Grat Younger organised this spy system, he was to be congratulated. It kept the settlers perfectly safe from any surprise — by day.

Several horsemen entering town from the east came around into the main thoroughfare riding slowly and, or so it seemed to Dan as he watched them, solemnly. He'd seen them before on the range; they were Gray Appleby's riders. They didn't see Dan, standing in the grey shade of his recessed doorway, and rode right on past, down to the federal marshal's office and tied up at the rack to troop on across and rattle the door. They wanted to see Fred Clampett.

Dan flicked his cigarette out into the roadway dust. They'd hit town a half hour too late. He stepped out of his doorway, went along to the café and had a good breakfast. Afterwards, with the sun high and the town humming with activity all around, he sauntered down to the liverybarn where there was a long bench bolted to the front wall under an overhang, and sat down to thrust his legs out their full length, tip down his hatbrim, prop both arms behind his head, and simply observe.

He saw those Appleby riders drift over to the Great Northern, but they weren't in there very long, before they came back out, stood a moment upon the plankwalk up yonder, gazing down at a neat little white-painted cottage with an equally as white-painted picket fence out front, then started hiking on over towards that house. Dan's interest increased slightly. The sign outside of that white-painted small house said: *David Lawrence, M.D.*

The Appleby riders were inside the physician's combination bachelor's quarters and office longer by far than they'd been over at the Great Northern. When they eventually returned to the golden-lighted, dazzling roadway, they had the doctor with them. He and one of the rangemen went briskly around back while the other men crossed over to the Great Northern's tie-rack, got astride and, leading one saddled horse, left town in a swift lope. Moment's later the doctor's top buggy spun out from behind his house through a narrow little alleyway, with the physician and that cowboy on the seat, and went rushing off in the same direction as the Appleby men had taken.

Dan speculated that someone out at the Appleby place had been injured; perhaps bucked off or trampled, or maybe gored. Those things happened around cow outfits. He saw Evelyn Benson come out of the general store, adjust the window-blind out front and go back inside. Just before she passed from sight through the doorway she paused to put a glance up and down the roadway. He thought she looked down in his direction for a moment longer than she looked elsewhere, and smiled under his tipped-down hatbrim, imagining how she'd wrinkle her nose with disapproval if she'd recognized him down there in the livery-barn shade.

The kinky-haired, paunchy hostler strolled out, squeezed sweat off his heavy features in the doorless wide roadway opening into the barn, and casually said, "Hot. Even gettin' hot in the early morning now. I'm a wintertime man, myself. Never did care too much for hot weather."

Dan swivelled a glance around at the man. He didn't look particularly mean or vicious up close; just fat and slovenly and a little sly. "It'll get even hotter," Dan murmured, eyeing the man and not entirely referring to the weather.

"I reckon," groaned the hostler. He turned and shambled back down into the barn and Dan swung back to watching the northern approaches to town. He had no intention of bracing Harper Todd's rangeboss again if it could be avoided at all, but on the other hand he'd been instructed to remain in town, and that made things a little awkward, because if there was one thing his superiors insisted upon, it was discipline. He'd been ordered to remain in Jefferson, which meant he'd remain, but no one had said he had to face Harper Todd's men either, so, as he watched and loafed, he also planned. There were a dozen excellent places a man could glide into, to avoid being seen.

It was close to noon when he saw them coming. Harper Todd himself was leading them, but they did not appear particularly war-like. In fact, they had an old spring-wagon bumping along through their dust as though they'd come to town for supplies.

There were eight of them, counting Todd, which meant every rider who worked for the older man, was mounted up around him. Dan watched them enter town, drew in his long legs, straightened up on the bench and thumbed back his hat. They'd pull in over at the general store, he speculated, and when they didn't; when they kept on riding down the main roadway, Dan stood up, hitched his shell-belt into place and edged over towards the entrance to the liverybarn where heavy shadows lay. He recognized Matt James among the cowboys behind Harper Todd. It was James who said something, directing the wagon and most of the riders to veer off in front of the physician's cottage where the wagon stopped. Harper Todd didn't dismount; he twisted in his saddle looking up and down the roadway. He was searching for someone. Dan thought he was looking for the medical man, but suddenly Todd turned his horse and started walking straight towards the liverybarn.

Dan had plenty of time to pass out of sight inside, but he was interested, so he remained where he was. Todd had seen him anyway. His men up there around the wagon were easing down the tailgate, but that was all Dan saw before Harper Todd's mounted figure blocked out his vision up the roadway.

Todd drew rein at the liverybarn hitchrack and fixed Dan with a blank look. "I'd like a word with you," he said quietly, not the least bit belligerent, so Dan stepped forth.

Todd loosened in his saddle and said, in the same inflectionless tone of voice, "Fred Clampett's up there in that wagon — shot."

Dan stopped in mid-stride, looking straight up into the older man's face. "Shot . . . ?"

"Through the body, Mister Miller. It's a right bad wound."

Behind him, Dan heard the fat hostler shuffle forward, listening. Todd ignored the man. Dan stepped sideways where he could see those cowboys up yonder carrying something limp on up to the doctor's front porch.

Todd said, "I found him. His horse was standing over him. Someone bushwhacked him down near the granite point; the place you camped night before last, Mister Miller."

Dan looked up again. "You accusing me?" he asked.

Todd shook his head. "I might have suspicioned you," he gravely stated, "but for one thing — while I was sittin' with Fred waitin' for the wagon to get back, he told me who you were." Todd gazed at the hostler briefly, then back to Dan again. "I reckon you'd better come on up there with me, Mister Miller. He's unconscious now, but I reckon he'll be comin' around when the doc gets to workin' on him."

"The doctor's not in town," said Dan, beginning to move, finally. "He went away with some of Appleby's men an hour back."

Harper Todd digested this and let his lips droop. "Fred needs professional help, Mister Miller; I tied off the bleedin' as best I could, but when a feller's gut-shot he needs more'n just bunkhouse patching." For a moment Todd sat in thought, then he brightened a little and lifted his rein-hand. "Evelyn Benson," he said. "I'll get her. You go on up there in case he comes around."

Dan paused to ask a question. "What about Evelyn Benson?"

"Back in her home town she was a professional nurse. Folks hereabouts've had occasion to use her too," replied Todd, completing his turn and heading back up the roadway.

Dan forgot about the hostler standing there in the barn's roadway entrance as he paced swiftly up the board sidewalk towards the doctor's house. He didn't speculate about the shooting either. Nor did he more than throw a glance at Matt James who was making a cigarette in the doctor's doorway, as he shouldered on inside the little building, jostled the solemn cowboys out of his way and entered the immaculate but small dispensary where they'd put Marshal Clampett upon a leather couch.

The bandaging was crude but effective. Fred Clampett was white in the face, his lips were fish-belly grey. He was breathing in a shallow, fluttery way and both his eyes were tight-closed.

Dan considered the blood-stiff bandage, thinking that Fred had lost a lot of blood. He was straightening up from this initial examination when Evelyn Benson swept into the tiny room accompanied by Harper Todd. She shot Dan a quick, troubled look, then firmly said, "Outside, please — everyone." He and Harper Todd walked out and Evelyn closed the dispensary door behind them. Four of Todd's silent rangeriders were in the anteroom with them. Todd motioned for them to leave. As they trooped back outside where Matt James was standing on the edge of the porch smoking, his back to the house, Todd turned and said, "Mister Miller; even if he pulls through, it'll be a mighty long time before he sits a saddle again." Todd kept studying the younger man. "It looks to me like you've got yourself quite a job, Deputy. Quite a job. Whoever shot Fred Clampett didn't do it accidentally, an' if shootin' one lawman didn't worry him any, shootin' the next one probably won't bother him a whole lot more."

Dan brushed this warning aside. "What else did he say, when you found him?" he asked.

"That was about the size of it, Deputy. He looked at me, recognized me and said for me to find you; that you were his deputy U.S. marshal."

"Anything about the man who shot him?"

Todd shook his head, felt around in a pocket and passed Dan a lopsided lead slug. "That's the bullet; it was lying under him on the ground."

Dan took the slug, hefted it, looked closely at it, hefted it one more time, then dropped the thing into a pocket. When he raised his eyes and gazed past Harper Todd, he saw Matt James standing out there on the porch, his steely grey eyes watching Dan behind their puckered-up lids, as cigarette smoke drifted in lazy spirals up the front of his face.

Dan fished in a pocket for his badge, brought it out and pinned it upon his shirt-front. The game of hide-and-seek was over,

66

but it hadn't been all wasted time and effort; he at least knew the countryside and most of the people who inhabited it. He walked out of the physician's house heading for the marshal's office. A lot of closed faces watched him go.

CHAPTER SIX

One hour later Harper Todd informed Dan he'd sent a rider out to Appleby's ranch with an order for the doctor to head right back because the U.S. Marshal had been badly shot. Only moments after Todd departed Evelyn Benson entered the dusty little gloomy office and put an arched look over where Dan was writing a letter at the marshal's desk.

"I owe you an apology," she said, not sounding in the least as though she were apologizing. "Although I think either Fred or you might have kept me from having to make it."

Dan stood up eyeing the very handsome tall girl. "How is he; what are his chances?" he asked her.

She gazed around the room as though it was her first visit. "His chances are very slight, Mister Miller. I think he would've survived the bullet, but a person can only lose just so much blood. After that, the process of replacement is too slow. The patient lingers, usually in a coma, then dies." She brought her smoke-grey eyes back to his face. "If I'm wrong I'll be delighted. I've known Fred Clampett a long while. He's a fine man."

"I'll agree," murmured Dan Miller. "Will he come round again?"

"Who can tell? I can't even say with any real accuracy just how much blood he's actually lost. But he has the appearance of a person who is bled out; skin colour, comatose condition, grey lips, sunken eyes, body coldness." She paused, passed back to the door and lay a hand lightly upon the latch. "He probably couldn't tell you anything anyway, Mister Miller. He was shot from a long distance off."

"How do you know that, Miss Benson?"

"The same way you'd know it, Mister Miller. Harper Todd told me he picked the bullet off the ground underneath Fred. Only a nearly spent bullet would have stopped after penetrating him like that, since it didn't strike bone."

She walked back outside leaving Dan gazing after her. He made a cigarette and smoked it, thinking some private thoughts, then he reached for his hat, went out onto the plankwalk, saw people standing in small groups here and there excitedly speaking, and sauntered down to the liverybarn.

The paunchy dayman was heatedly talking with an older, smaller man. When those two saw Dan approaching they turned silent, waiting for him to come on up. He sized up the wizened little elfish man, saw neither he nor the hostler wore visible sidearms, and said, addressing the hostler, "Mister; you're under arrest."

Both men blinked and gaped. When the paunchy man overcame his astonishment he said, "What for, Deputy? I ain't done nothin'."

"Maybe not," assented Dan. "But mister, when you heliographed those digger-pine watchers this morning that the U.S. Marshal was leaving town, you just may have become an accessory to attempted murder. You got a gun on you?"

"No, sir. But this morning I didn't ——"

"Save it," growled Dan, and reached. "Walk ahead of me. Make a wrong move and I'll render about thirty pounds of lard from your carcass."

The elfish, older man squeaked in protest. "Hey, you can't take him. I got to have help runnin' this barn. I can't do the work around ——"

70

"It'd be good for you to try," said Dan. "Or go up to the saloon an' hire yourself another hostler. This one's goin' to be on ice for a few days."

He drove his first prisoner up to the jail-house, locked him in, and crossed to Fred Clampett's desk to finish that report he'd been writing to the Territorial U.S. Marshal about the shooting of Fred Clampett, when Matt James opened the office door and ambled on in, a cigarette hanging from his lips.

Dan stood up. "You got something special on your mind?" he demanded. "Because if it's not important, James, I'm too busy right now to play any more games with you."

The long-faced gunfighter sauntered across the office and sat down. "I got a reason for bein' here," he conceded. "But before I get to that I'd like to tell you somethin' that's personal, between the two of us."

"Get it said, then get out of here," growled Dan, in no mood for duelling with words.

"Well; I didn't know you was the law before, when we met. Not that I'm scairt of the law, Deputy, but I just got a rule: Never buck the law."

"Is that all, James?"

"One more thing. I got no particular hard

71

feelings for what happened last night — now that you turn out to be a lawman." Matt stood up, considering Dan thoughtfully. "I hope you come out alive," he said, and ambled to the door, turned back and woodenly regarded Dan as he made his final pronouncement. "What they sent me down here to tell you, is that Gray Appleby's up there with the doc at his house — shot just like Fred Clampett's shot."

James walked on out leaving Dan standing there as though carved from stone. So that was why Appleby's men had come hunting the physician hours back! Dan left the office striding swiftly northward. There was a large crowd outside the doctor's place now, both townsmen and ranchmen. There were even a few digger-pine men mingling in the crowd. But there was no sign of Matt James until just before Dan went through the crowd up towards the physician's house. Matt was over across the way standing upon the overhang-shaded length of plankwalk out front of the Great Northern, with a glass of beer in his hand, impassively watching the crowd.

A thick-set cowboy stepped truculently forward as Dan headed straight for the door. The cowboy blocked his way, but when he saw the badge on Dan's shirtfront, he looked surprised. He was going to speak. Dan brushed him aside and entered the house. Harper Todd and several other men were in there, looking solemn and standing in strong silence. These men glanced at Dan as he went right on past, opened the dispensary door and closed it behind himself.

Evelyn Benson was there. So also was a dark, stocky, curly-haired, alert man who was working over Gray Appleby, and who looked up irritably as Dan entered. Doctor Dave Lawrence was normally an amiable enough individual, but this intrusion at a critical time made him brusque. He'd seen the badge, but it impressed him very little. "Marshal," he said, "wait outside."

Dan remained with his back to the door. He made no attempt to turn away. "Will Appleby live?" he asked, and the doctor slowly raised his dark face looking hostile.

"I am a physician, not a seer, Marshal. I don't know whether either of them will live."

"Have you found the slug that stopped Appleby?"

Doctor Lawrence rolled his eyes towards Evelyn. She picked something out of a small bowl, turned and held it out. As Dan came forward to take the flattened piece of lead she said, "Please leave, Deputy. I'll come down to your office as soon as I can. Right now you are a distraction. Doctor Lawrence is operating; he shouldn't be distracted." She kept looking straight at Dan while she softly spoke. She meant it, every word of it. He nodded, turned and went back out into the anteroom.

At once Harper Todd stepped out. "Is Gray still alive?" he asked. "What're his chances, Mister Miller?"

Dan was a long way off on a mental trail of his own and returned to the present here and now only after Todd had put out an arm to stop him from striding past. "Alive?" he said. "Yeah, Appleby's alive. They're operating on him. About the other question, Mister Todd — my personal reckonin' is that he's got a lot better chance than the man who shot him has."

Outside, that roadway crowd had thinned down a little, but there were still at least two dozen people out there whispering back and forth. As Dan walked out the little white picket gate a sun-reddened long-legged cowboy stepped up and said, "What's the news, pardner?" Dan eyed the man; he worked for Appleby. Dan shrugged and walked on past in the direction of his jailhouse-office building. Behind him a long-legged and red-necked cowboy made a grimace of hostile disapproval.

Dan still had that slug in his fist when he sat down at Fred Clampett's desk, leaned far back in the swivel-chair, and studied the thing. He didn't have to pry another carbine bullet apart to appreciate that the bullet in his hand which'd been taken from Gray Appleby's body was another of those rifle balls. He'd made that judgement the moment Evelyn Benson had dropped the thing into his hand up at the dispensary.

But what was especially bothering him was the matter of timing. Fred Clampett had been shot early in the morning over by that grey-rock headland. Gray Appleby had been shot by the same rifle, or at least by the identical *kind* of a rifle, a good ten miles to the north and east of that grey-rock headland. There wasn't a horse living that could put the same bushwhacker in those two places in so short a period of time, so of course, that meant there wasn't just one ambusher, there were at least two of them, both with rifles, not carbines.

Rifles were the exclusive weapon of the digger-pine men. What Dan and Fred Clampett had discussed the last time they'd secretly met, had been relevant to what had subsequently occurred. Someone was pushing for serious trouble between the hostile factions. Whoever he — or they — were, it did not look to Dan Miller as though too many of the digger-pine men were behind them; otherwise they'd have gone in a body to do their shooting, and not as one or two men skulking through the early dawn so as not to be seen by either side.

It appeared to Dan Miller that he had two, perhaps three or four, potential murderers to run down. It did *not* appear to him that *all* the digger-pine men were involved. In fact, if his theory was correct and only one or two men were involved in these ambushes, then it was highly likely that some of the digger-pine men were against bushwhacking. He'd had his chance to study those men before the shooting of Fred Clampett had forced him to reveal his identity, and although they were undeniably different in dress, customs, even in talk, from the cattlemen, he'd seen a number of them who looked to him to be self-respecting people, not back-shooters.

He dropped the bullet into his pocket, shot up to his feet and crossed to the doorway leading into the yonder small, stuffy room where the strap-steel cages were. The liverybarn hostler's name was Alf Dugan; he sat up off his bunk the minute Dan appeared, blinking owlishly in the poor light.

Dan said crisply, "I want you to tell me who the settlers over at Roan Mountain look upon as a good man among 'em, and don't tell me Grat Younger. Who's respected most, over there?"

The hostler gazed with strong suspicion out at Dan. "Why," he asked. "So's you can go make another arrest? Let me tell you somethin', Deputy, you're goin' to cause real bad feelin' goin' around like ——"

"Save the advice," snapped Dan. "Who's their most respected man?"

The hostler cogitated a moment and finally said, "Grant Withers. He's one of the original settlers. Folks listened to him up until they hired Younger. Now they listen to Grat."

"Grant Withers," repeated Dan. "He's that big old white-headed gaffer who lives smack-dab up against the mountain, isn't he?"

"He is," answered the kinky-headed man through his cell bars, "but don't be fooled by his age; he'll have you in his rifle sights three hunnert yards before you get near his cabin."

"One more question, Dugan: Did Withers suggest hiring Grat Younger?"

The hostler snorted derisively. "Not old Grant," he replied. "He was against it. Said hirin' a man like Younger'd only make things worse, an' that in a showdown the cattlemen could hire ten gunfighters to every one us settlers could hire, because they was richer."

"Withers was against fighting?"

"Well; he was against *that* kind o' fighting, Deputy. Ol' Grant said fight 'em legal in the courts, like happened when them surveyors divided up the Salt Lick. But when they come back an' re-surveyed the lick and changed the line, that's when the others got mad and hired Younger. After all; we lost a right good man when them devils killed Frank Talmadge."

Dan nodded, not in agreement with Dugan, but because he'd had a hunch there might be a division of opinion among the settlers. Otherwise, someone out there wouldn't be doing his damndest to force a serious fight; force *all* the settlers to support the few belligerent ones among them.

He returned to the office and was preparing to depart when Evelyn Benson walked in from the yonder roadway. She was composed and direct as always, eyeing Dan Miller with neither friendliness nor hostility, but with what looked to Dan to be a combination of both, or which could just as easily have been a combination of neither.

"Marshal Clampett regained consciousness a few moments ago," she told him in a voice as emotionless as her expression also was. "We asked if he'd seen the man who shot him. He said he hadn't seen him and didn't even know from what direction the shot was fired."

Dan nodded. He'd rather expected that to be the case. "How do his chances seem now?" he asked her.

"Doctor Lawrence said that if he can be kept entirely still and quiet for a week, and can be made to eat, he has a good chance of recovering."

"Fine. How about Appleby?"

"He died an hour ago without regaining consciousness, Deputy."

Dan hadn't expected that; it struck him like a blow. He felt around for his makings and instead came up with the flattened bullet which had come from the dead man's body. He stood staring at it. Evelyn watched him a moment, then softly said, "A rifle bullet, Deputy, not a carbine bullet." He looked up at her and nodded.

"Keep that to yourself," he told her. "So far, I think you'n I — and the man who fired this bullet — are the only ones who know that."

CHAPTER SEVEN

On the ride towards Roan Mountain, Dan kept turning in the saddle glancing back. He had the digger-pine-spy in jail, but that didn't mean there couldn't just as easily be another man back there prepared to signal the settlers when strangers were riding over towards their land.

But he saw no such signal. In fact he saw nothing at all, either from the direction of town or on ahead across the broad expanse of range he passed across before coming into the broken and up-ended digger-pine country.

Eventually someone would spot him, obviously, for the settlers seemed to be operating as though under siege. They had watchers out all around. But it didn't trouble him as he made his way overland towards Roan Mountain. He was several miles south of that grey-rock monolith where Clampett had been bushwhacked, but he nevertheless kept a cautious eye peeled for other ambushers. The closer he got to the cabins up towards the mountains, though, the less he thought he'd have any serious trouble, so eventually he turned to thinking of something else.

Those ambushers were now murderers. Gray Appleby had died. It was one thing to bushwhack without killing. It was something altogether different to kill a man from ambush. There was no way to mitigate such an act; it was murder pure and simple, with all the ramifications murder usually brings with it.

For instance, back there in town Harper Todd and the other Association stockmen would undoubtedly call an executive meeting. For another, whether anyone had any actual knowledge or not about how Appleby was shot, it wouldn't take very long for the rumours to start up, and they would have Gray Appleby drygulched by a digger-pine man in revenge for the slaying of Frank Talmadge. That was how range wars got started. Furthermore, the number of range wars which had been stopped by a solitary lawman could be counted on the fingers of one hand. Violence of this kind gathered its own blindly vicious momentum; even peace officers were not immune. Dan had no illusions at all, but neither did he propose to sit down and wait for the Territorial U.S. Marshal over in Boise to send him down reinforcements, in response to that report he'd written him, and which he'd posted just before leaving town. He in all probability couldn't halt what was impending, but he certainly couldn't even slow it down if he didn't at least make the effort, without awaiting reinforcements.

By the time he saw the Withers cabin tucked into a gentle fold in the brushed-off hills, he'd made his decision to do whatever he had to do, and if he failed at least everyone on both sides would have realized he'd given it the best he had.

He came across open country towards that yonder cabin and it was therefore inevitable that he saw, soon enough, that there was a rifle lying across the top tier of a woodpile over to the left of the cabin, shifting gradually as Dan advanced towards it. The livery-barn hostler back in town had warned him.

He took his time advancing, taking especial care that he made no movement which could be interpreted as hostile. In order for that man over there behind the woodpile to see that Dan was not bent on trouble, he made a cigarette for which he felt no need at all, but which kept both his hands well up in plain sight as he rode straight up to the hitch-post out front of the cabin, and halted. He gazed around, exhaled and said, "Mister Withers; if it'd been in your mind to shoot, you'd have done it long ago. And if there's anything useless in this world it's a gun that's not going to fire. I'm Deputy U.S. Marshal Dan Miller. I want to talk to you."

A grizzled grey head came up, over behind the woodpile, followed by a large-boned gaunt and slightly stooped big body. Grant Withers was probably somewhere in his sixties or possibly even his seventies, but obviously, at one time he'd been a man to reckon with; all the remnants and vestiges were still there to show that Grant Withers had been a powerful, oaken man in his time. He stepped around the woodpile, grounded his long-barrelled rifle and made a slow and deliberate study of Dan Miller.

"Talk," he said, making a command of it. "I'm listenin'. But if you come way up here because you figure I had somethin' to do with shootin' Marshal Clampett, you made a long ride for nothin', young feller. I haven't been off this homestead in ten days."

Dan took his time. He gazed around at the mean little outhouses, at the cabin itself, and he finally said, "Mind if I get down?"

"No," replied old Grant Withers. "Dismount and set, Deputy."

Dan swung off. Grant Withers made no move to come forward. He remained over by his woodpile leaning upon that old musket as though he were leary of Dan. There was an old grey-muzzled hound dog sleeping under the raised front porch. He hadn't moved nor opened an eye throughout all this. Dan said casually, "Your dog's a hard sleeper, Mister Withers."

"Deef," stated the older man. "Been deef four year' now." Withers faded, hard old eyes sardonically brightened just a little. "Like me, Deputy, m'dog's long in years. But he's had his day an' it was a good one."

"I'll bet it was," agreed Dan, and smiled. "You know a cowman named Gray Appleby, Mister Withers?"

"Yes. Not right well, but I know him. He runs stock over east of Jefferson."

"He's dead. Bushwhacked, Mister Withers."

Dan watched the surprise widen old Grant Withers's pale eyes and loosen the muscle down around his thin-lipped mouth. Dan waited, but the old man didn't say a word.

"Shot by a musket like the one you're holding, Mister Withers. The same kind of a weapon that downed Fred Clampett."

"Is Marshal Clampett dead too, Deputy?"

"No; but if he pulls through it'll be a miracle." Dan leaned upon the hitching post in front of the cabin, smoking and listening to the silence in this isolated, peaceful spot where Roan Mountain stood almost straight up out back and where a little fresh-water creek came down out of that farther back, uplands country, making scarcely any sound.

"An' you're lookin' for someone with a rifle; is that it, Deputy?"

Dan nodded. Old Withers lifted his musket and strolled on over. He eased down upon the porch steps nearby and let his solemn gaze drift down the lower country where it gradually sloped away. He had his rifle set aside where golden sunlight turned the brass fittings pale yellow in the brightness. Finally he said, "Well, Deputy; I predicted it. I been tellin' folks ever since Frank Talmadge got killed that we don't have the money nor the numbers nor the public backin', to fight no war with men like Appleby and Todd, an' all them other Association stockmen. I told 'em not to hire Younger; to spend that same money hirin' a fee-lawyer. I said sometimes the courts're fair enough an' unbiased, but there never was a gun that wasn't prejudiced no matter whose hands it was in."

"That was sound advice," murmured Dan. "Too bad they didn't take it."

The older man swung his head a little and gazed at Dan. "Yes," he said softly, "it was good advice, but they didn't take it, an' whether I like it or not, I'm on their side, Deputy. I wouldn't tell you which one shot Clampett an' killed Appleby if I knew — which I don't. The fact that a man don't approve of things don't mean he should turn traitor, does it?"

Dan dropped his cigarette and stepped upon it before raising his face to the older man and saying, "I reckon not, Mister Withers. But the reason I rode out here today was to ask you to go among them up an' down Roan Mountain and out through the digger-pine country; tell them not to let anyone sway them into fightin' a war with the Association men."

"I doubt that they'd listen, Deputy. They didn't listen the other times I talked to 'em. They banded together an' put up the money to hire Younger, didn't they?" Withers gave his head a little shake. "I'll do what you ask, but it'll be a plumb waste of time. If some of them shot Appleby an' Marshal Clampett, they'll be organized and ready. These folks are a long way from bein' dumb,

Deputy. They'll know what to expect from the Association men after those two shootings." Withers lifted an arm, pointing. "Look down-country a ways, Mister Miller; they're comin' up this way now. They saw you ride up here."

Dan straightened up off the post, turned and looked. There were six horsemen coming straight towards Grant Withers's cabin riding slowly and quietly, but with their rifles balanced across their laps. For several minutes the two men at the cabin watched. When they were within several hundred yards two of the riders veered off to the north, two peeled off towards the south, and the remaining two came up much closer before one of them halted back down-country a little distance, dismounted and stood leaning upon his rifle beside his horse, leaving just one man still aproaching.

"Younger," said the old man quietly, and reached for his own rifle, which he settled across his bony knees. "I'll handle this, Deputy. You stay out of it."

Dan had no such intention. He let Younger get within a couple of hundred feet before he turned fully towards the mounted man so that Grat Younger could see his badge. Younger saw it as he halted his horse and leaned forward in the saddle, gazing straight at Dan.

"I see you finally picked your side," the hard-eyed gunfighter said. "Let 'em swear you in as deputy U.S. lawman. Well; if a feller's got to be a lawman, that's the best outfit, I reckon." Younger shifted his attention to the older man. "Well, Grant; what's he been doin' — pryin' a little, maybe?"

Withers showed no fear at all as he steadily gazed up at the mounted man. He didn't answer Younger's query either, but said instead, "You put ten men together in a bad spot, Younger, an' you'll always find one who pushes real hard for a fight. I didn't know until this here lawman told me, that Gray Appleby was shot."

"Well, now," purred the gunfighter, smiling with his lips but not his eyes at the older man, "if you'd hitch up once in a while an' ride into town — or out to the salt lick — you'd know what's goin' on." With the same cruel expression Younger said, "Deputy; too bad about the marshal."

Dan nodded. "Too bad about Appleby too, Younger. He died. Marshal Clampett was still alive when I left town this morning. An' by the way; I threw your spy down there, Alf Dugan, into jail."

Younger didn't even blink, but when next

he spoke his voice was like velvet. "You're sure settin' out to make a name for yourself, Deputy, but sometimes fellers stub their toes. I'd go a mite easy, was I you."

"That goes two ways," replied Dan. "I can't prove you badgered these folks into those shootings, Younger, but if I ever do prove it, you're going to think the sky fell on you."

Now the gunfighter's smile disappeared. He leaned up there on his saddlehorn taking Dan Miller's measure, then he kicked his right foot out of the stirrup as though to dismount, and said, "Deputy; if you come up here today lookin' for trouble, you don't have to look no farther."

Old Withers swung his musket and cocked it. "Stay up there," he growled at Younger. "I've told you before, Grat, I don't want you on my land. Of all the bad things that've happened to us folks since we settled hereabouts, you're the worst."

Younger swung his free foot back and forth as though undecided, but in the end he put it back into the stirrup. No one in his right mind would start trouble with a rifle in the hands of a lifelong rifleman pointing directly at him. He said, "All right, Grant. But if words was to get around that you're workin' with this new deputy, there could be a right hot bonfire up here some dark night."

Dan's dislike of Grat Younger rose another notch. "If there ever is such a fire," he told the mounted man. "Even if you're over in the next county when it happens, Younger, I'll come lookin' for you."

The gunfighter's dark eyes narrowed the slightest bit. "You do that," he said, turning his horse to ride away. "You do that, Deputy. Don't wait for the bonfire, just you come for me any time you're in the mood."

Dan watched Younger ride back out where he'd left one of his companions, picked that one up, and ride on down-country until the other four joined him, then he stopped and looked back briefly before heading on towards the digger-pines farther along where he and his men were lost to sight.

Dan turned. Old Withers was putting his rifle aside. He said to the old man, "I sure didn't mean to get you into trouble by ridin' up here, Mister Withers. I only wanted to get someone they respected to try an' talk some sense into them before it's too late."

The old man gently smiled. "Hell," he said deprecatingly. "Son; I been in trouble of one kind or another all my borned days. *His* kind o' trouble is the least worst kind. I've seen a hundred like Grat Younger come an' go, an'

90

once or twice I've sort of helped them on their way." Withers put a direct glance upon Dan. "Sprout an eye in the back o' your head, Deputy. I don't know that he had anythin' to do with the shootin' of Marshal Clampett, but I *do* know that whoever did that's got his sights set on eliminatin' his most serious opposition, which in this case seems to be the law."

Dan stood a moment longer, then turned towards his horse, toed in and rose up to settle across leather. "I reckon I shouldn't have tried it this way," he mused aloud. "I reckon what I should've done was go after Younger straight off."

"And Matt James," suggested the old man. "He's cut from the same blood-red cloth, Deputy."

Dan nodded, threw old Withers a little salute, turned and went riding back down the open range. He didn't look back but he knew old Withers was back there, watching. He suspected Grat Younger of leaving a spy hidden somewhere to also watch, but he never saw the man. Never saw anyone, for that matter, all the way back to town.

CHAPTER EIGHT

There was a note on the desk when he returned to the office signed by Evelyn Benson, which said Marshal Clampett was conscious and wanted to see Dan. It was early evening by then, and since he'd had to postpone his noon meal this long, he went across to the café to take on a load of roughage. After that, he stood out front of the café having a peaceful smoke, and fitting some parts of his particular puzzle together. They didn't add up to much; he might feel confident Grat Younger had needled the digger-pine settlers into a couple of shootings, one of which turned out to be a murder, but not very many murderers had ever been hanged on the strength of some law officer's feelings.

He tossed away the smoke and strolled through the balmy, clear evening up to Doctor Lawrence's place, where he was taken in to see Fred Clampett by the doctor himself, who volunteered the information just before they entered the soft-lighted little room, that if nothing went wrong, Marshal Clampett would recover. But when Dan asked how long that recovery might take, the doctor only shook his head.

Fred Clampett was pale and weak as a kitten, but he was lucid and gave Dan a wan smile as the deputy drew up a chair and sat down. The doctor felt Marshal Clampett's pulse, bent over to make a close inspection, then straightened back and said to Dan, "Ten minutes, Deputy. No more."

The physician left them alone and Dan reported all that had occurred. The killing of Gray Appleby upset Clampett. He said, "Dan; you'd better go see Harper Todd. If there's a strike by the cowmen for Appleby's killing, Todd'll be the Association man who organizes it. You'd better go see the digger-pine men too."

"I did that today," said Dan, then decided not to tell Fred Clampett how that had turned out. "Had quite a visit with old Grant Withers. 'You know him, Fred?"

"Yeah," murmured the marshal. "Tough old coot, but fair and honest. He'd be the one to see, all right, unless Grat Younger's undercut him with the settlers."

Dan nodded, thinking his private thoughts

and turning the conversation to Harper Todd again. "How many men are in this Association, Fred, and can Todd influence them enough to make real trouble?"

"You bet he can," whispered Fred, looking earnestly at Dan Miller. "There are at least six cattlemen in the Association, an' I guess that if they pooled their men they could field damn near half a hundred guns. You've got to get to Harper before he gets carried away by Gray's killing, an' it just might not be very easy, Dan, because Harper and Gray Appleby were friends."

Dan's ten minutes were up. He got off the chair and gave Clampett an easy smile. "Don't worry," he murmured. "There won't be any range war if I can prevent it. By the way, Fred, Evelyn Benson said you didn't see the feller that shot you."

"That's right, Dan. I not only didn't see him, but it came so hard and fast I don't even know what direction I was shot from." Then Marshal Clampett seemed to remember something, for he said, "Was it another rifle ball, Dan?"

Miller nodded. He had that chunk of lead in his pocket but didn't bother fishing for it. "Same as Gray Appleby, Fred. I've got to hunt up Appleby's rangeboss and find out how Appleby got it, but I don't figure that's goin' to help me any; Appleby's dead and I know he was killed over on his own range, so all the rest'll have to be guesswork. What I'm really concerned with is — how many are mixed up in these shootings. If it was just one drygulcher I could eventually track him down, but —"

"You figure it's more than one bush-whacker?" asked Fred.

"It's got to be," stated Dan. "Appleby was shot at about the same hour you were, Fred, but he was shot over on his own range somewhere, which is roughly ten miles from where you got it. Unless that rifleman had wings and a stout tail wind, he couldn't have even gotten close to Appleby after he got you."

Fred let his eyes drift away from Dan up along the ceiling. Dan saw that, bent down to give the marshal's arm a light pat, then turned and left the room.

Outside, the curly-haired, stocky physician was waiting. He was drinking a cup of coffee and asked if Dan would also like a cup. Dan shook his head, replaced the hat atop his head and reached for the door-pull. Doctor Lawrence said, "Deputy; in case Evelyn didn't tell you today, Gray Appleby was shot from a long distance away."

Dan nodded; that jibed with the same

method used to down Fred Clampett. Then Doctor Lawrence said something that didn't jibe.

"He was excited and hot when he was shot, Deputy, otherwise he probably wouldn't have bled out so fast." Doctor Lawrence swished his coffee and watched it a moment before he looked straight at Dan and said, "My guess is that Appleby was running on foot when he was shot. Perhaps the killer had already fired at him and missed, or perhaps Appleby had seen and recognized the man, and was trying to run away from him. This is all pure speculation. All I can tell you of a certainty was that Mister Appleby was hot from exertion when he was shot down."

Dan gazed back at Doctor Lawrence for a long while, still holding to the door-pull. "On foot . . . ?" he eventually muttered. "What the hell would a cowman like Appleby be doing on foot way out on the range. I'd better ride out an' talk to his foreman."

"Save yourself some effort," said Doctor Lawrence. "He's coming in this evening with instructions for me about the body and the funeral. Mister Appleby had a sister and brother-in-law down in San Francisco. As soon as the foreman gets here, I'll send him down to your office."

Dan nodded and walked out of the house into the benign, warm night with its summertime fragrance and its faultless sky, speculating on how, exactly, Gray Appleby had been shot down. The mystery wasn't the assassin's identity, particularly; the mystery, to an ex-cowboy like Dan Miller, was the reason why Appleby had been on foot in the first place.

He strolled along towards the little building Fred Clampett had occupied, scarcely conscious of the people he passed, and who glanced at him with strong curiosity. He didn't even see the horsemen sitting out front of the office waiting for him until just before he reached the doorway and one of them said, "Deputy. . . ." Then he looked up. He was slow recognizing any of those six riders because of the dusk and the shadows, but when one of them stepped down and strolled over, he knew the man; didn't exactly *know* him, but knew who he was: The rangeboss for Gray Appleby. The husky, taffy-haired man thrust out his hand.

"Joe Flint," he said. "Appleby's rangeboss. We've seen each other before on the range, we just never met before."

Dan pumped Flint's hand and dropped it. "You been up to see Doc Lawrence yet?" he asked, and when the rangeboss shook his head Dan looked out where the other mounted men still sat. "Let 'em go on up to the Great Northern and get a drink, if you like. You can join 'em later, I'd like you to step into the office with me for a few minutes."

Flint turned and gestured. He didn't have to say anything. His cowboys swung, and went whooping up the road. Flint turned back, smiling. He was a young man, solidly made with a pleasant face and an open expression. Dan preceded him inside, lit the lamp and tossed his hat aside.

"Sit down," he said, and set an example by doing that himself. "I want to know who found Gray Appleby and where he was shot, and what the circumstances were."

"Sure enough," agreed Joe Flint. "I found him. He an' I rode up onto the north range about three miles to look at some greasy steers we'd put up there three weeks back to finish 'em on hard grass. Then we were goin' to —"

"Wait a minute," broke in Dan. "Do you know that grey-rock headland out where Fred Clampett was shot northwest of Jefferson?"

Fint nodded. "I know the spot well. We used to hold our roundups over there for

Association members who grazed on the west range."

"Then tell me, Joe, just about how far apart was the place where Appleby was shot, and that headland?"

Flint's expression turned mildly puzzled. "Hell man," he answered. "That's a dang good ten miles, between them two places."

"All right. Now go on with what you were tellin' me before."

Flint nodded, but it took him a moment to go back again in his mind. "Well; Mister Appleby an' I split off. He went over towards the foothills an' I cut off to the east. I figured I'd find most of those fat critters near a spring over there. I reckon about an hour'd passed when I thought I heard a gunshot."

"Just one gunshot, Joe?"

Flint said, "I'm comin' to that, Deputy. No; two gunshots. But they were a good fifteen minutes apart. When I was plumb satisfied they really *were* gunshots, I dusted it over in the direction the boss had gone. An' I found him over there, shot through, or dang near through the guts. He was unconscious. I went back to the ranch like hell on wheels to fetch a wagon. I also sent the boys after Doc Lawrence before I went back, got the boss and fetched him back to the house. I did what I could for him after we got ——"

"Did you see anyone out there where he was lying, or did you hear anyone?"

"Not a sightin' nor a soundin', Deputy."

"Where was his horse?"

"Gone. But there's somethin' I got to tell you about that which I couldn't have told you this mornin'. When the horse come home a couple of the men off-saddled it an' turned it out. It wasn't until after Doc arrived at the ranch an' took over that I had a little time on my hands, an' drifted down to the barn to check Mister Appleby's outfit. There was a bullet score across the rear of the cantle of his saddle, and slantin' down so's it ploughed across the rear skirts as well. I caught his horse and found where that slug had singed the critter over the rump."

Joe Flint stopped speaking and stared at Dan Miller. Dan nodded; he understood. That first bullet had missed the man but had stung the horse, getting Gray Appleby bucked off. After that the horse fled in one direction and evidently Appleby, knowing he was under personal attack by an ambusher, had also run hard trying to either find a suitable place to make a stand, or, failing that, to get as far as he could out of his attacker's range.

He might have been able to accomplish it except for one thing: The rifle that downed Appleby'd had a long barrel; there wasn't a man on earth, no matter how fleet of foot, who could out-run a bullet, when it was fired from a weapon with a range of about a mile, and which had apparently been in the hands of an accomplished marksman.

"Anything else?" asked Dan thoughtfully. Joe Flint shrugged.

"Not a whole lot. After he died I wired his kin down in 'Frisco. Meanwhile, I'll go on like he'd planned."

"I meant about the killing," stated the deputy. "Appleby's personal affairs don't much interest me."

"Well, no, I reckon not," said the range-boss, getting to his feet. "Except that later on today I rode back up there where he'd gotten it, lookin' around. 'Couldn't even find the ejected casings although I did find where a feller'd sat his horse for a spell, before gettin' down an' lyin' in the grass. But the tracks were hard to hold to, Deputy; I lost 'em a couple hundred yards off, to the north, where he went up into the rocky country of the lower-down foothills."

Dan also arose. "Thanks, Joe," he said. "One more thing: No matter how you feel personally, an' no matter what Harper Todd or anyone else says to you — don't get to pawin' and bellerin'. Appleby's dead. Marshal Clampett's down too. But there's not going to be any war against those digger-pine people over around Roan Mountain. If any of you cowmen try it, you're going to wind up about where Appleby is, one way or another."

For the first time since Appleby's range-boss had entered the office, his open, candid countenance, lost its frank look. He gazed at Dan Miller with a veil of blankness settling across his features. He turned, walked out of the office and didn't say another word.

Dan watched the door close, muttered a fierce curse under his breath, and had the answer to whether or not the other cowmen were plotting vengeance. Joe Flint's smoothed-out expression had given him that answer. *They were!*

He got supper for his prisoner on a tray at the café across the road, took it to Dugan and without saying a word returned once more to his office. He'd scarcely had time to make a smoke and lean back in the desk-chair to formulate some plans before the roadside door quietly opened and lovely Evelyn Benson entered. Dan got up out of his chair, nodding and closely eyeing the handsome woman.

She was as distant and poised as she always seemed to him to be. She had a taffy-coloured shawl around both shoulders and a white blouse beneath it. She said, "Deputy; Matt James just left the store with four of Harper Todd's men."

He nodded, not particularly interested.

"Matt James bought ten boxes of carbine ammunition and ten boxes of forty-five bullets."

Dan's awareness of the beautiful girl atrophied stubbornly but definitely at this news. He bent, stubbed out his cigarette, twisted around groping for his hat, then straightened towards her and said, "Which way did they ride out, Miss Evelyn, an' what did James say about buyin' so much ammunition?"

"They rode northwest, Deputy," she informed him in the same crisp, impersonal tone of voice she seemed always to use towards him. "And Matt didn't say anything at all except that he wanted that amount of shells."

Northwest would be back in the general direction of the Todd ranch. There was a chance, that was simply a replenishment of the ranch ammunition supply. There was, he wryly told himself, an even better chance those bullets were for the use of some secretly congregating Association men over at Harper Todd's place, who were rallying to avenge Gray Appleby.

CHAPTER NINE

It actually wasn't much of a ride out to the Todd headquarters-ranch, and with half a moon to light the way, plus a rash of pewter stars, Dan could have made it in good time except for the fact that he didn't ride directly to the ranch, and he didn't ride fast either, despite his personal feelings of urgency.

He knew perfectly well that if the cowmen were readying a strike against the digger-pine men over in the general vicinity of Roan Mountain, they'd have outriders scattered well ahead of their main column, watching for strangers, settlers — or lawmen. That was his reason for riding slowly and cautiously.

His reason for not heading straight for the Todd ranch was equally as elemental. If Matt James returned directly to the ranch after buying all that ammunition, he'd had plenty of time to get there, and the cowmen'd had plenty of time to get armed, mounted, and on the trail for Roan Mountain. Dan wasn't wild about intercepting perhaps fifteen to thirty armed and willing fighting cowmen by himself, but if he had an alternative he didn't see it as he came within sight of that grey-rock headland where he'd been accosted once before by the Todd-ranch riders, and where Fred Clampett had been shot down.

He didn't like making his interception in this vicinity either. He knew for a fact that the settlers kept this particular area under close watch during the day. There was a fair chance, after the recent shootings, they'd leave a man or two hereabouts at night, now, as well.

He was careful, stopping a half mile out to get down and put his ear to the ground, and after that, he was careful about riding within rifle — not carbine — range of that jutting old weathered grey rock.

The first clue he got that he wasn't alone in the ghostly quiet was when his horse abruptly threw up its head looking northward, which would be the direction Todd's men would come from. He stepped off and for the second time put his ear to the ground. That time he definitely picked up reverberations. There were a lot of them and they were coming slowly.

He got back astride, turning northward. It was his intention to ride boldly up and throw down on Harper Todd himself. The only way one man ever prevailed against an overwhelming number of other, hostile, men, was by boldness. As he turned his horse though, he didn't feel very bold, nor very brave. Still; he had this thing to do. He'd promised himself there'd be no range war if he could possibly prevent it, so, win, lose, or draw, he had to make this effort.

Off on his left less than a hundred feet a man rose up out of the grass. Dan saw him at once, but his horse was concentrating on the down-wind scent of the horses Todd's men were riding, and this time failed completely to warn him in time. He reined back and dropped his right hand. Off on that side and even closer, a man said, "Don't try it!" Dan swung his head. He was under that man's rifle too.

"I'm the deputy U.S. marshal," he growled, confident neither of those digger-pine men could see his badge yet. "Put down those rifles."

The settlers walked in closer to verify what Dan had said, but neither of them lowered his weapon. It was finally possible to hear the oncoming, walking horses, moving down-country steadily and all bunched up. One of Dan's captors looked over his shoulder. When he looked back again he was savagely grinning. He said, "Deputy; we been waitin' since last night. We knew they'd be comin' one of these nights."

"Let 'em come," said Dan, angry with himself more than with his captors. "That's why I'm out here. To stop this before it gets started."

The other settler, a big, stooped, coarse-featured man with small, steely eyes and a drooping set of lips, shook his head up at Dan. "You ain't goin' to stop it," he muttered. "They killed Frank Talmadge; they been worryin' us day'n night out at the Salt Lick. They think they own the world. Well; tonight they're going to find out that's all hogwash. They don't own nothin'!"

Dan eyed this settler stonily for a moment, then leaned to dismount. At once the surly one said, "You stay up there, Deputy. Maybe if they see you first they'll come right on in."

Dan disregarded that order and swung down. Both the settlers stepped around his horse with their rifles levelled. He said, gazing at the tough-faced other man, "Go ahead an' shoot. That's all it'll take to break up your bushwhack. You might as well shoot, boys, because if you live through this tonight you're both goin' to prison. I'll be the Territorial witness against you for deliberately ambushing unsuspecting riders in the darkness."

The surly, small-eyed digger-pine man wasn't touched at all by that promise, but his companion shifted a little, alternately glancing over his shoulder in apprehension, and eyeing Dan Miller. Clearly, this man hadn't bargained for bucking the law as well as the cowmen. He finally said, "Come on, Wheeler; let's get t'hell out of here while there's still time."

The surly man barred his teeth when he answered. "Not on your life we don't run. Why; jes' the two of us can lay down four, five of them lousy cowmen — and this deputy marshal — an' we can do it so's it'll look like the cowmen killed this lawman, not us."

Dan turned his head, wondering if there were any more settlers lying hereabouts in ambush. The disagreeable man named Wheeler saw that look and chuckled. "Ain't no more right here, Deputy," he stated. "But back a mile to the south'n west they're a-waitin' in the rocks an' trees jes' like we was waitin' in the grass. Them cowmen'll leave a heap o' widows this night —

109

a-skulkin' along like they're tryin' to do, an' catch us settler-folk unprepared. Deputy; we jes' ain't never been *un*prepared since they kilt Frank Talmadge. Since that Appleby feller an the other lawman got ____"

"Shut up, Wheeler," gasped the other digger-pine man, badly shaken by what Wheeler was revealing. "What's the matter with you?"

Wheeler turned and smiled. "Nothin'," he said. "Hell; like I said, this lawman's goin' to die right where he's standin'. So what's the harm in him knowin'?"

Dan heard the oncoming cowmen clearer now and guessed they couldn't be more than a thousand or two yards away. In the half-light of that tilted moon up there, they'd very soon now be in sight. He groped for something to distract his captors with, and said, "Wheeler, you're a damned fool. Did you think I came up here to stop a war all alone?"

Wheeler at first sniffed, then, when the other settler straightened up to look around, Wheeler licked his lips and darted a look back down the night in the direction Dan had come from. That wasn't much of an opportunity, but Dan had no illusion that he'd get a better one, so he yanked his horse half around to shield most of his body, streaked for his sixgun and fired across the saddle-seat at the same time Wheeler ripped out a wild curse and yanked his own trigger. The gunshots were almost simultaneous; almost but not quite, and that was invariably what made the difference between a living man and a dead man.

The bullet Wheeler fired peeled the horn-cap off Dan's saddle, striking within five inches of the deputy's hatbrim, but Dan's bullet struck flesh and bone with an audible ripping sound, and Wheeler threw up both arms and staggered backwards. The other settler tried to get positioned to also fire, but Dan had him lined up in his front sight before the man was even close to firing. Dan aimed low that time, breaking the man's leg just above the right knee and dropping him with a great cry of agony in the grass.

Wheeler fell, finally, and grunted back there in the grass at the same time he beat the ground with his feet and his fists.

The silence which ensued was bottomless and endless. It sang down the night with a wire-tight hush that stretched far beyond where the startled and astonished cowmen back up there were sitting their horses, unprepared for the kind of trouble which had exploded down the night from them.

Dan led his horse on over and looked down where Wheeler lay. The man was dead. He went over where the other settler was sitting up, his grey face beaded with sweat, holding to his bloody right leg and gasping through clenched teeth in terrible pain. Dan emotionlessly gathered up their weapons, flung them far out through the darkness, stepped aboard his horse and reined up in the direction of the cowmen.

They saw him coming at the same he saw them sitting up there. They covered him with guns from the left, the right, and from dead ahead. He picked out Harper Todd and headed straight towards him. While still a hundred feet out he said, "Now tell me you an' this mob of idiots riding with you are out huntin' strays in the dark, Harper Todd."

The older man made no answer to that. He didn't say a word until he'd recognized Deputy Miller, who reined up twenty feet out and dropped his reins staring straight at those bristling, wary riders. Todd finally loosened a little in his saddle, cleared his throat, and said, "What was that shooting about down there, Mister Miller?"

"I killed a digger-pine man, Mister Todd, an' I winged another one."

Todd's brows knitted. "Ambush . . . ?" he

asked softly.

Dan shook his head. "What did you expect, ridin' towards Roan Mountain in this direction so soon after Appleby's been shot? Mister Todd; the wonder to me isn't that these simpletons riding with you let themselves be talked into this; the wonder to me is that you've lived as long as you have."

The cowmen glanced back and forth at one another. They put up their guns and glumly watched Dan Miller dismount and stroll up beside Todd's horse on the left side. Somewhere down where that gunfire had erupted a man's choking groans were audible. That had an un-nerving effect too.

Dan said, "Mister Todd; you're very lucky tonight. There were two videttes down there who could've cut you to ribbons without any help, but there are more of them farther along, also waiting. They'd have probably wiped you out down to the horses you're sittin' on. Now take these other damned fools back to your ranch, disband them, and tomorrow morning you ride into Jefferson. I'd like to talk to you when we have more time."

Dan stepped back. Harper Todd looked more uncomfortable than wrathful. He said, "Deputy; we'd best say what we got to say right here an' now."

Dan saw Matt James, back from Todd a few yards, ease his right hand down his right side. Dan said, without raising his voice, "I'll put one squarely between your eyes, Matt, if you try it." At the same time Dan stepped in closer to Harper Todd again, caught the cheekpiece of the cowman's bridle and turned his horse regardless of rein-pressure. "I won't tell you again," he said. "Ride back the way you came an' don't stop nor turn back." He removed his hand from the bridle. "Todd, listen: You hear those riders out there comin' from the south? Those are more digger-pine men. They heard the shooting too. Now move out!"

It wasn't Harper Todd who finally led the cowmen back up-country, it was one of the other ranchers. There were several of them, along with their rangeriders, in Todd's armed force. Todd checked his horse up close, leaned from the saddle and said, "All right, Deputy; I'll see you in the morning in town at your office." He still didn't look wrathful, but Dan Miller got a mixed reaction to his expression and those final words he uttered. Harper Todd wasn't quitting just because a deputy U.S. marshal had gotten the drop on him, any more than he was quitting because he heard those digger-

114

pine men approaching. He had something else definitely in mind. Men like Harper Todd didn't give up until they stopped breathing.

Southward, a man's anguished outcry sounded. Dan knew who that was and surmised from the fact that the wounded man had cried out, that he'd seen friends coming. Dan had known the digger-pine settlers would eventually appear after that fierce and lethal little gunfight down there. He also knew that this was not the time for him to ride back down there and deliver his ultimatum to the settlers, as he'd just done with the cowmen; the settlers had two casualties down there; it was very improbable that they'd listen before they'd shoot.

Dan mounted up, sat a moment listening to the distant, small sounds of those settlers down there finding their dead companion and his wounded associate, then turned his horse and started slowly back towards Jefferson. It was quite late, he was tired, all the tension of the earlier hours had drained him, and as he poked along now, he'd have handed over his interest in the whole Jefferson countryside to anyone naïve enough to take it.

He'd prevented the fight, true, but without any illusions about what he'd really ac-

115

complished, he knew very well all he'd done was affect a temporary truce. Todd's cattlemen wouldn't stop just because he'd saved them from an ambush, and the digger-pine men, with two more casualties — one dead — would be more than ever anxious for vengeance.

He hardly thought those settlers, with Grat Younger to egg them on, would differentiate now between the cattlemen of the Jefferson countryside, and the lawmen. Both had killed settlers.

He saw the town lying low upon the southeasterly plain, silver-mantled by the descending moon, and idly rambled in his tired thoughts. If the Territorial U.S. Marshal over in Boise decided Dan Miller's report merited credence, he'd send down another deputy or two. If not, or if, because he was chronically short-handed in his territory, he decided to do nothing for a while and see how things developed, he just might have to come to Jefferson himself — with a larger force — and bury a deputy marshal along with policing a countryside which was now well along towards the very strife Dan had wishfully hoped to avert.

He rode into the liverybarn, tossed his reins to the nighthawk, turned without a word and went striding towards the U.S.

Marshal's office. He never quite made it. From some heavy shadows southward of the office, a moving silhouette glided out calling him softly by name. It was Evelyn Benson.

CHAPTER TEN

She said she'd been waiting a long time and he believed her. It was midnight, the town around them was silent and lifeless. The moon was down but the stars still cast their ancient light, soft-turning now that the small hours were approaching.

He asked her into his office but she declined, saying she'd prefer to stroll as they talked, and he let her set their course and their gait, which was slow, and which was also out through the easterly section of town where dark residences stood in opposing ranks across the broad dirt roadways from one another.

"It is hard to sleep," she told him, walking with her head slightly down, her creamy profile towards him. "I was the one responsible for you going out there tonight; it troubled me that you might be killed."

"Well, I wasn't," he told her. "So you can put your mind to rest about that."

"Not tonight," she retorted, looking swiftly over at him. "But it doesn't end there, Deputy Miller. We both know that. Doctor Lawrence and I discussed you today. Putting on that badge made a target of you."

"That's one of the risks of my trade," he said, very conscious of her nearness and her powerful desirability. So aware, in fact, that his earlier weariness dropped away entirely. He only generally noted the course they were taking, which led eastward out towards the edge of town. "I killed a man tonight, Miss Evelyn. A man called Wheeler. One of the digger-pine settlers." He stopped and turned. "I also wounded another one. It was that, or be shot down during an ambush of cowmen. It was a lousy choice to have to make, but there was no way out."

"Wheeler . . . ?" she murmured. "Carl Wheeler?"

"All I know about him is that the other one called him Wheeler. I never heard his first name. He was a sulky, string-bean of a man with a strong Southern accent and a sour expression."

"Carl Wheeler," she repeated, only making a statement of it this time. "That was Carl Wheeler. He was one of the men who sent for Grat Younger. He's been troublesome ever since he came out here."

"I see. Did he have a family?"

She shook her head, turned and continued to slow-pace the bland night easterly. "No family. But he was a friend of Younger's, Deputy."

"Thanks for the warning," he murmured.

She stopped again, swinging straight towards him. "You have to either organize the local men or send for more peace officers, Deputy. Killing Wheeler changed things; this won't be just a war over the salt lick any more. Not now."

"Ma'am," said Dan quietly, looking her straight in the eye, "it never was strictly a war over the salt lick. It's been a feud between oldtimers and newcomers right from the start. The salt lick just happened to be where first blood was spilt."

She stood close, waiting for him to say more, but he didn't. He loosened a little and gave her a lopsided small smile. This was the first time since he'd met her that she didn't show him the cool, poised side of her nature. She was troubled now, and anxious; it showed in the darkly shifting depths of her grey eyes and in the quick rise and fall of her breasts. He didn't delude himself; it wasn't for him personally that she was upset. It was for the perilous future and what she saw was inevitably going to come out of all this.

He said, "Evelyn; if it'll make you rest easier — I've already sent for another deputy or two. I'm not sure I'll get them. Idaho is a big territory; the head office over in Boise only has twelve men to police the entire area. But I can tell you one thing: No one has yet shot a deputy U.S. lawman and lived to brag about it. An' no one's got away with starting a range war in Idaho either, although a few have tried it."

"But that's all afterwards," she said, speaking so rapidly she blurred all her words together. "What good will it do if you're dead and if a dozen other men are killed, Dan; what possible triumph can either side claim if soldiers or federal officers ride into Jefferson to invoke martial law and scour the countryside hanging men?"

He stepped around her to lean upon a picket fence and quietly say, "Evelyn, whether it does any good or not, you and I aren't going to be able to stop it now. I thought for a while there might be a way, but after what happened out there tonight I know a damn sight better. Both sides have lost men, not just to each other, but also to the law. From here on it's not going to be a private feud; folks are goin' to choose sides."

"Yes," she bitterly agreed, "and with the

law in the minority, not separate and in the right."

He shrugged. "I could've stood there and let Wheeler shoot me," he said. "It wouldn't have changed anything. In fact, Wheeler and his friends would then have gone after the cowmen. There wouldn't have been just one dead lawman, Evelyn, there'd have been maybe four or five dead cowmen and some dead digger-pine men. The law, tonight, acted in the only way it could have acted. Right or wrong, it stopped the bigger fight."

"And signed its own death warrant," she retorted.

He stopped speaking for a moment; stood there gazing at her. Cool and poised or troubled and upset, he'd never in his life seen a woman who affected him the way she did, and she seemed oblivious to this other thing, or at least he thought she was oblivious to her effect upon him. Then she softly said, "A man's duty, Dan, is to live and make a better world, not die just because he won't take a backward step."

He felt around for his tobacco sack and fell to making a cigarette. He lit up, eventually, exhaled and said, "Evelyn; that's not right. The only good that's ever come to this world has come through suffering and blood. It may not be the right way, and perhaps someday that'll change, but until it does men — and women — will go right on dying for what they know is right. If everyone took a backward step from trouble, pretty soon there wouldn't be anything *but* trouble." He straightened up off the picket fence and turned as though to walk on again. She reached, caught him by the arm and pulled him around.

"Dan — they'll kill you!"

He considered her grey eyes, nearly black now with sudden and naked concern, and her alluringly close, heavy mouth. "At least it won't happen tonight," he murmured, and reached for her, let both hands grasp her at the waist pulling her to him. At first she seemed to stiffen, to resist instinctively, then she let herself be drawn in. He saw the quick, stark fear shadow her face, and dropped his head down cutting out her view of the stars and the quiet night all around.

He was gentle, touching her lips with his mouth softly, supporting her body against his, but without any demanding pressures. She responded the same way, at first, then her passion flamed at him; she pressed close their full length and held him to her by both shoulders. He was just starting to respond the same way when she suddenly pushed clear and backed away, turned without being willing to meet his gaze, took his right hand and tugged.

He let her lead him along for a hundred feet before he stopped, pulling her down to a stop also. "I reckon I've wanted to do that since the first time, in the store, when we saw each other."

She said, still not looking at him, "Has it always been that way in each strange town you go to, Dan?"

He was a little shocked at that remark. "It's never been quite like it has here, Evelyn. A man walks through a corral full of good horses and one stands out to him. He'll never forget it. Or he sees a thousand sunsets, but one particular sunset lives ever after in his heart. He knows he'll never see another exactly like that one. Or — he rides into a place like Jefferson and sees a woman; he'll never see another like her as long as he lives. Something deep down tells him that is so."

She looked up, finally, her eyes misty, her lips soft-tilted towards him. "For a stubborn man," she murmured, "you have a way of saying the right things. It probably won't keep you alive any longer, Dan, but it'll always make people remember you."

He smiled at her as they walked on, hand in hand, each lost in a poignant world neither could ever really share except if their relationship became even more intimate, unmindful of the time — it was now close to two o'clock — and unmindful of what had initially brought them together this night, until they halted, finally, where the roadway trickled off into twin dusty ribbons which ambled out over the star-washed yonder plain and disappeared out there somewhere, heading always easterly.

"Evelyn," he said, "it would've been better if this hadn't happened tonight."

She squeezed his fingers. "I know. But a good memory, Dan, even with sorrow, is better than no memory at all."

He looked down at her. For a woman, she was perceptive, even, in some ways, very understanding. He'd known his share of women; what man of his virile age with his striking looks hadn't; but he'd never known one like Evelyn Benson before. He felt a sort of pride of possession for her. She was very lovely. She was also knowledgeable. Perhaps he'd live to wonder whether that wasn't an unrealistic combination in a woman, but standing there in the soft night considering her creamy beauty, the notion didn't cross his mind.

She turned. "We'd better go back."

They returned through town by a different little back roadway, Evelyn leading him because he didn't have any idea where she lived. At the gate of her aunt and uncle's dark residence she placed both hands upon his chest, raised up and kissed him fully on the lips, then dropped down and stiffened her hands against him when he'd have reached for her.

"No more," she softly told him, near to smiling up into his eyes. "We've both had enough for one night, Dan. Maybe even too much."

"What does that mean?" he asked, puzzled by her suddenly changing mood and sad gaze.

"I'm not so sure I can weather the sadness which might go with the memory after all," she whispered. "Tomorrow they'll have made up their minds about you on both sides. The odds terrify me."

He took both her hands and said, "Tell me something, Evelyn; was it simply because you felt responsible for sending me out there tonight that you waited down there for me to come back to town?"

She shook her head. "Not entirely, no. But I wasn't willing to believe the — other — reason right then, either. Dan; I've never been in love before. I wasn't sure that's what it was. But I knew I had to see you, talk to

126

you. And I suppose I also had to be close to you to verify that other feeling." She withdrew her hands, passed inside the gate, closed it and leaned briefly upon it looking at him. "I don't suppose that makes much sense, does it? But I'm not a man and you're not a woman; we'll probably always fail to completely understand each other." She leaned towards him. He kissed her once more with the gate between them, then she turned and ran up to the porch and entered the house.

He stood out there for a while running a lot of confusing things through his mind and coming up with no genuine answers at all except the one fact which he fully recognized: He was in love with Evelyn Benson.

But that wouldn't have been hard to plot from the first time he'd seen her. He knew that as he turned and went strolling back up towards the centre of town. Somewhere, some time, every man meets his Evelyn Benson. It was a Natural Law that this should be so. But what troubled Dan Miller as he rounded the corner up northward of the Great Northern Bar, which was hushed and dark now, was the simple fact that when a man found his Evelyn Benson, his circumstances probably were as bad as they'd ever been in his life.

Not just financially either, but also in the way the cards had fallen for him the day before — rather, the *night* before. What she'd said had been undeniably true; the coming fight was no longer exclusively between cowmen and digger-pine men; it was a three-cornered contest with Dan Miller the Deputy U.S. Marshal, in the third corner, out-numbered, out-gunned, out-planned.

He paused out front of the hotel where he had a room, to make a cigarette and slouch against an upright post smoking it. Down at the liverybarn where two lanterns burned he could make out the nighthawk slumped down in a folding chair with a cowhide back and seat, sound asleep with his hat tipped down over his face. Elsewhere, there wasn't a soul stirring or visible. Westerly, far out where shadows lay upon an ancient mountain and down over a melancholy series of breaks and upthrusts and patches of scrubby digger-pines, there would be men awake, sitting with the dead and their wounded.

Northwesterly too, it was very probable other men were sitting around an oilcloth-covered kitchen table drinking black coffee and examining their fingernails, the toes of their boots, and one another's faces.

Whatever decision these two factions arrived at would determine Dan Miller's fate. Of the two, he expected direct violence from the digger-pine men, and indirect action from the cattlemen. He'd broken up all their plans this night, and he'd done it mercilessly.

He dropped the cigarette, stepped upon it grinding it underfoot, hauled up off the upright and cast a final slow look out and around, then went into the lighted hotel lobby feeling tired again, and troubled, and for some reason, also a little light-headed. He went up to his roadside room and stood for a moment beside the window. He could see the general store across the roadway southerly. She worked there. He went to his bed and sat down. Matt James had also bought twenty boxes of bullets there. Whatever tomorrow held, he was positive he'd have reason to recall both those totally unrelated facts, kicked off his boots, removed his shell-belt, tossed aside his hat, lay back and instantly fell asleep.

CHAPTER ELEVEN

Harper Todd appeared in town just shy of noon, with Matt James riding beside him. Dan Miller had breakfasted, had visited Fred Clampett up at the physician's place, and had even had a minute to stroll into the general store and smile at Evelyn, before heading on over to feed Alf Dugan, his prisoner. Dugan was articulately indignant; he was, he loudly protested, being treated like a dog, getting fed whenever the deputy happened to remember he was locked up, and otherwise totally ignored, when he hadn't really done anything except warn his friends when possible trouble might be coming their way.

Dan didn't argue with him; he simply shoved the tray of food under the cell door, returned to the outer office and when Harper Todd and Matt James walked in, he was dropping down over at the desk to write up his report of what had happened the night before. He nodded at Todd and James, motioned them to seats across the room, swung to gaze at them, and waited. Harper Todd had the grievance, if there was to be one aired this morning. At least Dan preferred to view things in that light. His own grievance could wait. It wasn't actually against the cowmen anyway; it was against Grat Younger as a result of what Carl Wheeler had boasted about before Dan had killed him. But Dan didn't mention that to anyone. For the time being he preferred keeping his own counsel about that matter.

Todd said, "Deputy; you didn't make me look very good last night."

Dan's answer to that was blunt. "I wasn't trying to. I'd just shot two men to keep you from making an even bigger fool of yourself, Mister Todd. Since then I've been turning over in my mind whether to lock you up or not."

"Lock him up," growled Matt James, beginning to look vaguely hostile. "We didn't do anythin' last night, Miller."

Dan gazed at James thoughtfully, then launched into an explanation Matt James had probably never heard before. "A crime," Dan said, "consists of two parts: Intention and commission. Without both, a crime isn't generally considered a felony. But with one or the other, it's considered enough of a breach of the peace to warrant arrest and confinement."

James sniffed. "What's that mean?" he asked.

"It means I can lock your boss up — and you along with him — for *intending* to raid the digger-pine settlement."

Matt subsided. He was out of his element in this kind of a discussion. It clearly made a vague kind of sense to him, but the kinds of arguments he was accustomed to had very little to do with actual legality, beyond the strictest adherence to that basic tenet of law which made it plain a man could only kill another man in fair fight in his own defence. Matt knew just that much law, and no more, but he wasn't alone in that; Harper Todd leaned back looking down his nose at Dan Miller both sceptical and respectful.

Todd said, "I won't deny that was our intention, Deputy. We had the right. They killed Gray Appleby yesterday."

"Where's your proof of that, Mister Harper?" Dan demanded. "By now you also know I killed one of them, a man named Wheeler, last night. But you couldn't prove I killed him."

"You said you killed him, yourself," retorted the cowman. "What's better'n a confession?"

"A *written* and *signed* one is better, Mister Todd, an' no one has that kind of a confession from the digger-pine men about Appleby. Until someone gets that kind of a confession you have no more right to lead a mob of armed cowmen over there than I have — or than anyone else has. Now you have a choice; your word you won't try that again, or go to jail. It's up to you and I don't figure to wait around here all morning for your answer, either."

Matt James put his cold gaze upon the deputy. He did not now look like the same man who'd offered, in an oblique manner, not to cross Dan Miller the day before. Beside him, Harper Todd sat and thought and finally said, "My word won't stop the trouble, Deputy. Every man who was with me last night is just as fired up for trouble as I am — as Matt here, is."

"Matt," said Dan, "turns his indignation on and off, for a price. So does Grat Younger. Their kind understands just one thing: A gun that's faster than their guns."

"You think you got it?" James asked.

Dan stood up. "Matt; once before you pushed for a showdown. That other time I had other things on my mind. Today I've still got other things on my mind — but stand up an' we'll see which is the fastest gun."

James leaned as though to arise but Harper Todd threw out a restraining arm. "Hold it," he exclaimed. "Deputy; this won't settle a damned thing. Whether you're faster or not, I'm not goin' to have Matt shoot a lawman."

Dan was gazing straight down at James when he softly said, "He wouldn't do it, Mister Harper." Dan didn't amplify that statement; he left it for each of them to figure out whether he meant Matt couldn't beat Dan to the draw, or whether he meant Matt wouldn't draw against a Deputy U.S. Marshal.

As he resumed his seat, Dan said, "Time's run out, Mister Todd. Either give me your word or your gun. Either you walk out of here sworn not to lead another raidin' party of cowmen, or you walk through that door yonder into a cell."

Todd stonily regarded Dan Miller. "You're different from Clampett," he muttered. "All right, Deputy; I'll lead no more raids — unless *they* raid *us*. A man's got every right to defend himself."

"Get himself butchered, you mean," growled Dan. "Last night you were in a fair way of gettin' into every newspaper in the country like General Custer did — by being a damned fool."

"Whoa," exclaimed Matt James, angry all over again. "Mister Todd did exactly what anyone else would've done under the same set of ——"

"Shut up, Matt," exclaimed Dan, getting to his feet one more time, striding over and opening the roadside doors. "One last piece of advice to the pair of you: When the Association meets again, don't push for trouble. If there's another attempt at retaliation over Appleby, I'll bring in enough other federal lawmen to put you down and keep you down — all of you." Dan jerked his head indicating the interview was ended. Matt arose but Harper Todd sat there a moment longer steadily regarding the youthful Deputy U.S. Marshal. Miller had derided Todd, called him down, snarled at him, ordered him to go contrary to his own wishes, and was now telling Todd to get out of his office. Todd arose, eventually, hitched at his gun-belt and followed Matt James out upon the sunlighted plankwalk. He turned and looked back, his tough, uncompromising blue eyes oddly enough, without either anger or malice.

"Miller; I wish you luck," he said quietly. "They'll kill you before day after tomorrow

135

for what you did to them last night. But by gawd I wish you luck. We may never be on the same side, but I understand your kind of a man a sight better than any other."

Matt and Harper Todd went out to their horses, got astride and trotted up towards the Great Northern Bar. Dan stood in his doorway watching them, his eyes warming a little, his tough-set jaw relaxing. He thought he understood the kind of a man Harper Todd also was. He was dead-certain he understood the kind of a man Matt James was.

The sun wasn't quite at the meridian when he went down to the liverybarn and got his horse. That same elfish old livery-man did the bridling and saddling; he was just as sulky and resentful as he'd been the day before when Dan had arrested his hostler. Not a word passed between them.

Dan left Jefferson riding due west towards Roan Mountain again. He was going after Grat Younger, but he had no illusions about his reception by the digger-pine people. The man with the broken leg would certainly have identified Dan Miller as the killer of Carl Wheeler. Still; he'd braced one faction, so now he also had to brace the other faction.

It was slightly past one o'clock before he

saw the pair of motionless horsemen atop their little scrub-oak knoll, watching him. When he got closer he could also see their long-barrel rifles balanced athwart their laps in the saddle. He loosened the little leather tie-down on his forty-five and headed straight for those sentinels.

The settlers let him come right up to within twenty feet of them without moving or speaking. When Dan stopped and asked who they were watching for, one of them replied with a perfectly blank and hostile face, saying they were keeping watch in the event the cowmen came down from the north.

"You're facing the wrong way," said Dan. Both the settlers were looking towards Jefferson. One of the men, a youthful, sturdily-built person with a mop of unruly blond hair sticking out around an old battered felt hat, shook his head at Dan.

"We got reason to be watchin' in your direction too," he said flatly. "You're with the cowmen."

Dan eyed those two. They were hostile to him without making any hostile moves about it. He could understand their hostility; after all, he'd done what the cowmen had attempted to do the night before; kill settlers. "Where's Younger?" he asked them, and saw the veil drop down over both their faces. They gazed at him without answering for so long he repeated the question.

"I asked where Grat Younger is?"

"Maybe at his homestead," said the older of those two digger-pine men. "Maybe anywhere, this time o' day."

Dan wasn't going to get any more out of those two. He eased his horse out around them and went down the far side of the knoll back to relatively flat country again. Once, far out, he turned to gaze back. Both the digger-pine men were hastening down off their knoll and spurring up-country out and around him. He watched their dust for a while, sardonically speculating that they'd have the entire countryside alerted to his presence shortly, which meant he'd be intercepted again before he reached the Younger claim.

He was right. Close to two o'clock coming around the final bend in the rutted trail leading to Grat Younger's place, he saw them fanning out around him like Indians. They had their rifles and were obviously hostile, but like the first two settlers, they didn't appear bent on forcing a fight. At least not right then.

They'd evidently come from up along Roan Mountain's lower slopes, and from the southerly territory as well, from the way they were converging on him, yet staying a fair distance off.

He'd noticed the other time he'd ridden up in here that these people had their own unique way of accosting a man. It was exactly as the Indians had done, too. They let a victim see them, appreciate their strength, estimate their armament as well as his own chances, then they had just one man ride down to palaver. Ordinarily, with cowmen at least, the approach of hostile men was all in a belligerent rush. Fights started and ended in the same manner. These settlers were altogether different in their hostile strategy.

When he finally got far enough around the slope to see the Younger place, they had cut him off in front and on both sides. He had no illusions about withdrawing; they'd be back there too.

He selected one trio of motionless horsemen up ahead on the wagon-road and made straight for them. As the others had done, these men let him walk right up without moving or speaking, and also like the others, when he halted to address them, they kept their right hands on their balanced rifles, gazing straight over at him with open and candid looks of hostility.

"I'm looking for Grat Younger," he told them, recognizing only one of them as a man he'd seen before, farming a poor patch of gravelly foothill soil over closer to Roan Mountain. He didn't know the man's name; all he knew from spying on the digger-pine area, was that he had his hundred and sixty not far from old Grant Withers' place, and had a scrawny wife and two half-wild little children, both boys.

The other two settlers were cold-eyed, lanky men, looking both cruel and hostile now. Their horses were notched just forward of the withers from collars; obviously they were combination animals — used both for saddle as well as harness work.

The man Dan recognized said bleakly, "Grat ain't at his claim, an' I'll give you some decent advice, Dep'ty: Turn your horse aroun' and ride back just like you come. It's not right healthy for you up in here today."

"Be glad to take that advice," replied Dan, "when I've talked with Younger."

"He ain't aroun'," the bleak man repeated. "He won't be good for you to see, nohow. You killed a good man last night, an' you crippled up another good man so's his kin'll have to work out 'cause he can't put in no crop on one leg."

Dan said levelly, "Mister; I stopped a massacre last night. I'd stop one again, if I could. Your dead friend had me already dead an' the blame for my murder fixed on the cowmen. I didn't have a damned thing to lose, drawing against his cocked rifle."

"You were lucky," one of the other settlers growled. "Just plain lucky, Deputy. Ain't a man livin' who could've done that against Carl Wheeler 'less he had more luck'n any man's got a right to."

Dan glanced briefly at that man, then back to the bleak-eyed man directly in front of him. "Luck or not, Wheeler asked for that, and he got it. But I don't have to explain anything to you fellers; you were probably with the other bunch waiting for the cowmen so you could complete the massacre. Boys; what happened last night isn't going to happen again. That's one of the things I want to tell Younger. Now; where can I find him?"

The settlers exchanged a glance, then the one Dan recognized said, "Dep'ty; Grat went with four wagons and twenty-five men to the Salt Lick. We got an order to ship more block-salt. If there's any cowmen out there too. . . ." The bleak-eyed man thinly smiled. "Dep'ty, we'll just see whether there's goin' to be another massacre or not, an' whether you're man enough to stop it, too." The settler jerked his head, turned and rode away.

CHAPTER TWELVE

The possibility of reaching the Salt Lick from where he'd discovered why Grat Younger wasn't in the hills, in time to stop trouble, was out of the question. He'd have to return to town, get a fresh horse, then start the overland ride to the Lick. All that would take a lot of time.

Of course he could've pushed his saddle animal hard reaching town, secured a fresh beast and pushed on again for the Lick just as swiftly on the next animal, but all that would accomplish would be to put him at the Lick long after any serious trouble had already been resolved with guns, if, in fact, there was going to be any trouble out there.

What he finally did, was ride back down towards town at a little jog, alternating that jog now and then by boosting his beast over into a lope. He didn't make good time; at least he could have made better time if he'd chosen to wind-break his horse.

He wasn't willing to do that. Furthermore, as he rode down the golden daylight a touch of bitterness inspired him to reflect that as far as he was concerned right then, those cantenkerous cowmen and digger-pine men weren't worth ruining a good saddlehorse over.

Later, approaching Jefferson, he also blamed himself for an inability to be in two places at the same time. It had never crossed his mind anyone, settlers or cowmen, would be out on the salt flat.

He got a fresh animal and left town heading northeastward. Two miles out he spotted a brace of riders loping in the same direction he was riding, but those two were a goodly distance to the northward; if they saw him they gave no indication at all of it.

When he saw another horseman, this one coming down-country from the direction of the Salt Lick, heading loosely in the direction of town, he detoured a little to intercept him. It was this man who verified Dan Miller's worst fears.

The cowboy was one of Harper Todd's men. He stopped for Dan and held up a blood-spattered left sleeve with his left arm in a neckerchief-sling.

"Took one right through the muscles," he said, grey-faced with discomfort. "They sure caught us flat-footed, Deputy."

Dan was a little sceptical of that. If the digger-pine men had gone to the salt field to quarry, which they'd obviously done since they'd taken four wagons with them, it was hard to imagine they'd gone just to catch the cowmen flat-footed. But, if the ambushers had been cowmen, not settlers, it would sound more reasonable.

Dan said, "Who's leading the cowmen out there?"

The rangerider was cautious about replying to that. "Well; there's a bunch of fellers out there, Deputy. I can't rightly say who the leader is. We was fillin' a wagon when they come down on us like a whirlwind."

"I suppose they attacked you over on the cowmen's side of that survey line Marshal Clampett established," said Dan.

"Sure did," agreed the cowboy. "We was mindin' our own business, diggin' out there in the damned heat, when they hit us like a ton of lead. I stopped one right off. Matt said for me to head for town and get patched up by the sawbones."

Dan nodded. "Go on, mister," he said, and rode away from the cowboy thinking that he was heading straight for a show-down with Matt James.

He was still a long mile away with the

countryside beginning to flatten out, to turn alkaline and sere, and blazing hot as well, when he heard what seemed like the faint and far-away popping of corks being yanked from bottles. It wasn't a constant thing, though, which made him think that either the battle was dying, or that it had settled down to an exchange between snipers.

He eased his animal over into a slow lope, held him to it until he could distinctly make out the flat sounds of gunfire and the softer sounds of gunshot echoes, then he slowed to a fast walk again.

It was breathlessly hot out here. There was no shade short of some blue-blurred distant mountains. Nothing grew upon the edge of the salt field except a sickly kind of saw-edged grass, sometimes called ripgut, and while visibility should have been excellent, it wasn't for the simple reason that out in the sink the alkali turned to pure white salt, which reflected sunlight and made it impossible for a man to keep his eyes wide open. The glare was especially bad this time of day.

Dan felt his horse strike the first crisp rind of salt as he entered the salt field. Now, those onward gunshots were becoming fewer and farther between. The battle, evidently, was nearly finished.

He had to skirt great holes blasted in the salt field. There were ruts from iron-tyred wagons criss-crossing the Lick. There were also shod-horse marks showing where horsemen had come and gone. Between rains this crusty place took every impression and held it indefinitely; it was next to impossible to tell a fresh track from a very old one.

But Dan was riding by sound, and by the general knowledge he'd piled up during that week he'd had to familiarize himself with the countryside, before Fred Clampett had been shot down. He knew where the latest diggings were, and rode straight towards them.

The firing stopped altogther. The Salt Lick resumed its normal hush. Small animals did not usually come to this place so there were no birds to break the eternal silence, no crickets or frogs or other chirping small creatures. On a moonlit night the Salt Lick was as desolate and eerie as the dark side of the moon.

But this was broad daylight, although it was getting along towards late afternoon, so the silence seemed all the more oppressive. Long before Dan saw the first two wagons west of Fred Clampett's demarcation line, he knew where the cowmen were. He'd spotted a little bunch of horses off to the west being guarded by one mounted man. From a half mile off and despite the white-hot glare, Dan saw that rider and knew from the way he sat his saddle that he wasn't a settler. The man also spotted Dan, but evidently didn't recognize him because he made no attempt to signal back over to where his friends were holed up beneath their two wagons.

To the east, but a very long way off — so far off in fact that he could scarcely make out their wagons — were the settlers. But what he specifically sought he didn't find: Armed men from one faction or the other over across the line of demarcation. He'd obviously arrived too late for a first-hand view of who was being attacked and who were the attackers.

As he rode up closer Matt James crawled from beneath a wagon. Matt's shirt was dark with sweat, he'd tipped down his hat to protect his eyes as much as possible, and he looked both wrathful and uncomfortable. The moment he recognized Dan Miller he started to swear.

Dan rode on up ignoring Harper Todd's rangeboss. He bent to gaze into the wagons. One was full of chunk-salt, the other was partly full, and on the ground around the jagged hole where the cowmen'd been digging, were their scattered shovels and crowbars. There was no denying that they'd actually been quarrying salt when the fight started.

He reined back and gazed around the area. There were nine men including Matt James. Counting the one he'd encountered on his way to town to have his wound cared for, there had been ten cowmen out here. He could tell by their clothing and the way of their general appearance that they'd been digging salt. He told them to put up their guns and get back to work, after he made sure there were no more injured men among them, then, with Matt James's indignation still ringing in his ears, he started on across the survey line towards those four distant settler-wagons.

It was a goodly little distance he had to cross, and inevitably, long before he was within hailing distance, they had seen him coming. Four of them got astride and, brandishing weapons, charged out towards him. Dan eased off the tie-down on his forty-five and kept right on, heading straight for the wagons. When the four agitated settlers swirled on up, recognized the Deputy U.S. Marshal and began to haul down to a stop, he met their sulphurous glances with a cold look of his own and waved them back the way they'd come, with his left hand.

"Go on back," he told them. "You've had your fun for today."

Perhaps it was his clear determination, or perhaps it was his appearance of deadly efficiency, but in any case, the four men turned their horses. One of them called over, saying they'd been peacefully quarrying salt when the rangemen had charged them. Dan's reply to that was wordless; he gazed bleakly at the speaking man and made that same little peremptory gesture again, only this time with more solid emphasis. The settlers had no more to say.

Grat Younger was waiting in the lean shade of one wagon. He and Dan traded a look, then the deputy marshal rode in close to the wagons, leaned from his saddle to look inside, and afterwards gruffly ordered all the men to stand clear so he could see how many were hurt.

None were.

Younger's dark gaze never left Dan for a moment. When the others stepped away from their wagons, Younger remained with his shoulders in the lean shade of a wagon's grey side-boards.

There were twenty-five of them, all armed with their rifles and also with belt-guns. For a change, too, they were well-mounted; each

150

man evidently had brought along his best saddle animal.

Younger said, "Miller; they hit us without any warning. We'd just drove 'em back over on their side of the line before you come up."

Dan gazed across the shimmering, intervening distance. There wasn't a bush, a rock, a tree, anywhere around. He lowered his glance. "You must've been workin' awfully hard, Younger, for ten men with two wagons to get out here without you once sighting them when they had two miles of salt flat to cross before they even got to the line. And after that, for ten men to charge you on horseback, you'd also have to have been plumb deaf not to hear 'em coming. Every step a horse takes on this salt-crust sounds like a stick breaking underfoot."

Younger's eyes narrowed the slightest bit. Otherwise he didn't change nor move. He was holding a rifle in his left hand; his right hand was loosely hanging within inches of his hip-holster. "You callin' me a liar?" he asked.

Dan shook his head. "I don't have to call you one, Younger. You just did that for me. And Younger — don't. . . . Just leave it in the holster. You'd never get it out anyway."

"No?"

"No!"

The settlers dripped sweat and stood stiffly out there watching. They were armed the same way Grat Younger was also armed, but they didn't appear to have the same degree of iron; or perhaps they'd already had all the fighting they wanted. In either case, not a one of them seemed prepared to draw on the federal law officer.

"This'll prove to everyone," growled Younger, "whose side you're on, Miller, tryin' to make out like us settlers started the fight."

Miller jerked his head sidewards to indicate their wagons. "Your tools haven't even been unloaded," he said. "There's no salt in the wagons." He paused to let each of them catch the drift of his accusation. "You're riding your fastest horses. Boys; you knew the cowmen were coming down here. Probably one of your spies saw them pulling out with their wagons. I won't swear to that, but I'll swear to it that you caught up your best horses, hitched up and made a fast run to get out here on the Salt Lick too."

"You're sayin'," muttered Grat Younger, "that we deliberately forced this fight. Is that it, Miller?"

"That's it, Younger. I'm also saying something else, too; every damned one of you is under arrest. Now you can go ahead and make a fight out of it, or you can throw those guns into the wagons and go back to Jefferson with me as prisoners of the law."

"You're askin' for it," said Younger, finally straightening up off the wagon. "Miller ____"

"Easy," murmured Dan very softly to the professional gunfighter. "I warned you before, Younger. You'd never get it done."

Younger was confident. He said, "You're the biggest damned fool I ever seen, Miller. There are twenty-five armed men in front of you, not countin' me. If you figured that tin badge'd save your bacon, you sure guessed wrong this time."

"The tin badge," said Dan, "*and* Matt James over there with his nine rangeriders, *and,* all the federal lawmen in Idaho Territory, if needs be, *and* two hundred troopers from Boise, if that's also necessary, Grat, but you're not going to win no matter what you do right now."

Among the copiously perspiring settlers, several men looked at one another and shuffled their feet uneasily. What Dan had quietly said was no idle boast and they knew it. From the corner of his eye Grat Younger saw his men beginning to weaken, to lose their taste for what was impending. Younger himself stood balanced upon the knife-edge of an irreversible decision — whether to draw or not to draw against the Deputy U.S. Marshal.

Younger never had to make that decision; one of his digger-pine men stepped away from the others, walked over beside a wagon, pitched his rifle inside and drew forth his sixgun to do the same with it. Another settler, head down and shoulders slumped, also walked over and flung his weapons into a wagon. Two more went over and disarmed themselves, then, in a reluctant, grudging line, nearly all the others did the same. Grat Younger'd had the decision made for him. Very slowly the stiffness went out of him. He looked around, found himself nearly alone, looked back at Dan and dropped a fierce curse.

Dan said, "All right boys; the rest of you toss your guns into the wagons, too, then mount up and let's head for town. The jail won't be big enough, but we'll worry about that when we get to Jefferson."

Over across the demarcation line Matt James and his riders walked away from their wagons to stand staring as four wagons and more than twenty disarmed digger-pine men started plodding overland in the direction of Jefferson. Where the two parties

154

crossed within easy hailing distance of one another, the silence went unbroken.

Riding behind the wagons, alone and with no gun in his hand, was Deputy U.S. Marshal Dan Miller, hatbrim tugged low, shirt front soggy with sweat, his sun-layered dark face showing none of the grim resolve one might have expected under the circumstances. He turned, gazed over where the cowmen were dumbfoundedly standing, and passed along without even nodding to them.

The digger-pine men were across the salt field and upon the roundabout alkali flat before Grat Younger let his horse drop back. When Dan came up beside him Younger said in a very low tone, "Deputy; back there you dug your own grave. You can't hold us, and as soon as this is over, I'm comin' for you."

Dan looked across at the older, darker man, and thinly smiled. "I doubt that," he said. "You had your chance back there, Grat — and your guts oozed out through the soles of your boots."

"You're wrong, Deputy. I didn't lose my guts. I just didn't want twenty witnesses is all." Younger lifted his reins and spurred on up ahead leaving Dan to gaze thoughtfully after him. What Younger had just promised was a bushwhack; a bullet in the back!

CHAPTER THIRTEEN

Dan's entry into Jefferson made local history. Men and women tumbled forth from stores, houses, even saloons, to crowd up along the edges of both plankwalks, watching.

At the general store, Evelyn Benson stood in a window. Over upon the opposite sidewalk, Doctor Lawrence came out to stand upon his little white porch, also staring.

There were some cowmen in town. They whooped. Farther along, down nearer the jailhouse, there were also some of the digger-pine men, including tall, gaunt, and stooped old Grant Withers. They were glumly silent and doggedly watchful.

When Dan called for the rigs to halt, for their drivers to climb down, the entire cavalcade was out front of his jailhouse. Rangeriders rushed up gleefully. Dan stopped them with one tough pronouncement.

"Get the hell back away from those men! I didn't need your help out where the fight was and I sure don't need it now. Get back there on the sidewalk and stay there!"

The cattlemen obeyed, but looked a little gritty about being sworn at like that. Harper Todd was there, in the forefront of the roadside crowd. He called over to Dan asking what had happened. Dan told him in a few terse words as he swung down and pointed at his office door, herding his captives inside. Todd started shouldering his way through to Dan. The cowman was anxious. Until Dan explained about the Salt Lick battle, no one, apparently, had any idea what had occurred, or where.

"Deputy!" called the cowman, elbowing on up the last fifty feet. "Miller! What about my riders? I sent them out for salt to take up onto our north ——"

"You've got one man shot in the arm," said Dan, turning in his doorway. "He's probably around town here somewhere. At least when I saw him he was heading this way to get patched up."

"The others . . . ?"

"All right. Mad and sweaty, but able to cuss a blue streak."

Todd reared back shooting Dan Miller a savage look. "I kept my word," he said.

"And look where it got me! My men shot up and one hurt, by that unwashed scum in there. All right, Deputy — the damned worm's going to turn. Forget that promise I made you. I'm going to ——"

"*Todd!*"

Dan's voice cracked like a whip. All the lesser voices in the crowd went silent. All those faces lifted quickly; there was no mistaking the meaning of that voice.

"Todd; you so much as recruit one rangeman, or even so much as look crossways at one settler, and I'll be after you, money marbles or chalk!"

Dan stood framed in the office doorway, totally unsmiling, totally willing to back up his last words. He meant exactly what he'd just said. No one, including Harper Todd, doubted that for one moment.

The prickly spell lasted until someone up the northward roadway sang out, and the crowd shifted its attention. Matt James, his two wagons and his riders were entering Jefferson from the same direction Dan and his twenty-five captives had also entered it. The crowd began to break up, to surge ahead up towards this latest entrance into town of a battered, fight-scarred group of horsemen. Harper Todd turned away also, but Dan caught him, forcing him back around with cold, slow-spoken words.

"Todd; I meant what I said. You push this after giving me your word you wouldn't push it, and I'll be after you without any damned legal papers at all, because this isn't just a law-matter to me any more. It's personal; I'm takin' it that way from here on. Personal, Todd, and you can tell Matt James that, too. As for your promise, Todd, you'll keep it or I'll kill you!"

Dan went on inside, slammed the door on Harper Todd and looked around. Those digger-pine men had all heard his exchange with Harper Todd. Even the ones who didn't like him, which was to say over two-thirds of his prisoners, seemed less certain about him now.

Only one of them was smiling; that was Grat Younger. He drawled, "That's the way to handle 'em, lawman. That's the only talk them cowmen understand."

"That goes for you too," said Dan. "Bush-whacker!"

Several of the digger-pine men stiffened. One of them rolled up his eyes and moved his lips. Dan made a mental note about that one. But actually, Dan had been referring to Younger's private threat back out on the trail before they all got into town, not, as that solitary settler evidently thought, about the ambush-killing of Gray Appleby. At least that's the interpretation Dan put on that man's startled, frightened reaction when Dan called Younger a bushwhacker.

Younger hung both thumbs in his shell-belt looking down his nose at the Deputy U.S. Marshal. "You're crowdin' your luck," he said quietly, his hostility coming up again. "Deputy; you're sure crowdin' your luck. Just because we decided to let you bring us in today don't mean you really got any o' us buffaloed. Don't push too hard or you're goin' to find out how wrong you are.' "

Dan removed his hat, tossed it upon Fred Clampett's desk and pulled a paper out of a drawer. He handed it to the first man on his left, along with a gnawed stub of a pencil. "Put down your name," he ordered, "then pass the paper around. Every man write his name down."

As the settlers started complying Dan faced Grat Younger again, taking the gun-fighter's slow, careful measure. He'd never, right from the beginning, meant to lock all these men up. In the first place the two cells in the back room wouldn't begin to hold them all. In the second place he wasn't convinced that was necessary. There were a few tough-faced, mean-eyed men among

161

them, but generally, those men were defiant and vengeful more than either cruel or naturally vicious.

He had no illusions, either, about one man being able to cow an entire countryside. What he had in mind was simply to neutralize the worst men of both factions, then try reasoning with the others. He had an idea that if he could wean the troubled settlers away from their war-hawk leaders, he still might be able to prevent wholesale warfare. Right now, standing in that small and crowded room exchanging hostile stares with Grat Younger, the idea seemed both weak and improbable, but he'd pulled Matt James's teeth in front of the cattlemen, and now he meant to do the same with Younger, in front of the settlers.

The paper came back full of scrawled signatures. He put it on the desk and pointed to several of the more craggy digger-pine men, picked up his cell-keys and pointed towards the door leading into his cell-room. "You boys come with me," he ordered. "The rest of you stay right where you are."

For just a moment it looked like there might be trouble; one of those settlers balled up his fists and glared his defiance. "You ain't lockin' me up in no cowman-jailhouse," he snarled at Dan.

The deputy didn't answer right away. He crossed over, unlocked the oaken intervening door, flung it wide, drew his forty-five, pointed it and cocked it. "You want to say that again?" he softly asked. The settler didn't want to say it again; he was still defiant, but he trooped on inside right along with the others. He didn't speak another word, either. Dan locked them in, some in the same cell with Alf Dugan, the others in the other cell, then he returned to the office, leathered his gun, flung the keys on his desk and went to the roadside door to open it. He left his hat lying on the desk.

"Outside," he ordered. "Line up out front of the jailhouse, boys, along the front wall. *Move!*"

There were sixteen of them; they obeyed without comment, probably as glad not to be locked up as they also were bewildered at what they'd been ordered to do. But they were obedient; they strung out along the front wall of the jailhouse like soldiers, unarmed, perplexed, demoralized. The last man to saunter out was Grat Younger. He threw Dan a gritty smile as he passed through the door. Dan didn't smile back. He let Younger get five feet ahead, then stepped forward, caught Grat by the shoul-

163

ders and rushed the astonished gunfighter straight out across the sidewalk and hurled him out into the manured roadway.

There were several small groups of idlers on both sides of the roadway, watching. They snapped up, aghast, as Younger fell and rolled, kicking up clouds of dun dust. The settlers lined up outside the jailhouse, were equally astonished.

Dan walked out into the roadway and said, "Get up, Younger. So far you've been doin' all the tough talking. Now let's see you back it up."

Grat got onto one knee looking over at Dan. His brown eyes were like wet, dark stone, his heavy hands were relaxed, one upon the ground, one lying loosely across his bent knee. Younger understood, finally, what Dan had in mind. He licked his lips, ranged a glance at the settlers watching from over in front of the jailhouse, and he slowly drew both lips away from his teeth.

"You can't do it," he said. "One of us is goin' to get humbled in front of witnesses, all right, Deputy, but it won't be me."

Younger catapaulted himself forward; he'd been talking like that only to get Dan off-guard. Dan stepped in, brought up his right knee and caught Younger flush on the jaw snapping his head violently backwards.

Younger fell back. Dust flew and across the road a man let off an admiring hard oath.

Grat rolled, got up onto the same knee again, and studied Dan. He had been hurt by that unexpected knee-strike. Dan gave him plenty of time to recover. Younger finally pushed off the ground, stood over into a low crouch and began circling. He didn't smile now, nor say a a single word. He was deadly serious.

So was Dan; part of his overall strategy had to do with shaking the settlers as well as the cowmen down to their boots. He'd already done that by knocking Matt James senseless. He had to do it now with Younger to achieve the same uncertainty among the digger-pine men. He turned, keeping face-forward, and when Grat flicked out a long arm, Dan took the stinging little strike up alongside the temple without attempting to spring clear.

He let Younger flick two more of those little stinging jabs at him, then he went suddenly sideways as the gunfighter jumped at him, swung from the belt and rocked Grat with a jab of his own.

Younger went back again, flicking in and out with those little jabs. He had his shoulder rolled up, his chin tucked into its fold. He was no novice at this kind of brawling,

165

obviously.

Dan started in. He got under one jab, rolled with another, and knocked aside the third one to make his own hard strike. Younger tried back-peddaling. Dan went after him the second Grat was on the defensive. He cracked the gunfighter under the ear, sledged a blasting strike into his middle, straightened him up with a vicious, short little uppercut, missed with a hard right and was deflected by slippery blood from Younger's cracked lips when he tried for the knock-out punch to the chin.

Younger stumbled backwards and got away. Dan could have gone after him but he was content to stand off surveying the damage. Blood dripped; Younger's eyes were misty. He opened and closed his fists in a lethargic kind of half-stupor, but he was still willing.

There wasn't a sound now. Both sides of the plankwalk were crowded-up with men, cowmen as well as townsmen, and also a little sprinkling of the long-rifle settlers from over around Roan Mountain. One of the latter, rawboned, gaunt, and stooped, watched the systematic destruction of Grat Younger with grim pleasure: Grant Withers.

Dan started forward one more time. Younger shuffled his feet and raised his hands, but he was too groggy, his timing was too badly impaired. Dan hit him in the belly, over the heart, smashed him in the mouth again, straightened him up with another of those cruel little uppercuts, then chopped him down with a savage blow to the head on the left, and a blasting blow to the jaw, on the right.

Younger went down. A trickling dark stain spread through the roadway dirt beneath him. Dan wiped his hands and looked over along the front of the jailhouse. Those settlers were dumbfounded.

"Get him out of here," Dan told them coldly. "And I'll remember you. If I see another of you with a rifle in his hands more than a half mile from your claims, you'll get the same. Now get him out of here; go on home, and *stay there!*"

CHAPTER FOURTEEN

When evening finally arrived the town was buzzing with talk. Up at the Great Northern Bar the cowmen wagged their heads over that beating they'd witnessed, saying that unless someone challenged Dan Miller with guns he was going to whip half the countryside with his hands. Several of the men eyed Matt James askance, but Matt had nothing to say about having also been whipped by Miller. All he or the men who'd been out at the Salt Lick with him discussed was the way those digger-pine men had jumped them, out-numbering the rangeriders two-to-one.

"And those damned rifles they got," James declared, "could reach a mile. No wonder we never hit any of 'em. There's not a Winchester saddle-gun made that can even begin to shoot like that."

"But there are pistols," someone said, hinting by this remark that if the cowmen'd go after the settlers, in a close-quarters fight they could thin them down considerably, for none of the digger-pine people were as fast nor as experienced with forty-fives as rangeriders were.

Harper Todd, standing thoughtfully with several other Association members at the bar, shook his head about that. "Wait," he said. "We'll just wait. There's no chance under the sun that Miller can do what he's tryin' to do. But we'll wait nevertheless."

Matt raised his eyes. "Why?" he asked. "Why wait, Mister Todd?"

"Because, Matt, if those settlers kill Miller we'll have the legal right to form up a big posse, including all the townsmen we'll need, and go after them."

Matt and the others thought that over and began to smile a little. Todd was right; if the only law left, after Dan Miller's death, was lying half dead over at Doctor Lawrence's place, then it would be the duty of the rest of the community to mete out justice.

Matt said, "That's right good, Mister Todd. Right good."

Down the road across the way at the dingier saloon where the digger-pine men met, it was said that Dan Miller wrote his own one-way ticket to hell when he thrashed Grat Younger as badly as he did. There

169

weren't very many digger-pine men still in town; all those whom Dan had ordered back to their claims — and Grat Younger — were no longer around.

Old Grant Withers, stooped as always, but nursing a glass of tepid ale down at the far end of the bar, said in his deep-down, rumbling voice, "You're a bunch of damned fools, that's what you are. I *told* you an' *told* you not to waste good money hiring a gunfighter. Now look around an' see what it's got you. Trouble, men; trouble any way you turn, and *we* won't benefit. Grat Younger will though, because you have to go right on payin' his murderer's wage."

One of the tough-eyed men said, "Grant; you're talkin' like an old man. Them cowmen're layin' for us since the killin' of Appleby an' the shootin' of that federal marshal. You can't no more bargain with a rattlesnake than you can ——"

"Rattlesnake," snorted the old man, turning his indignant, wrathy gaze towards the speaker. "Younger's the rattlesnake. He's goin' to get half a dozen or so of you killed, if he has his way. An' that Matt James the cowmen've got, he'll do the same for his side. All those men care a holler in hell about is keepin' all this stirred up. They make a lot of money every week they can

go on drainin' us an' drawin' their wages."
The old man stamped his feet, plunked down a coin beside his half-emptied beer glass, turned and went stalking out of the saloon. Behind him, some of the digger-pine settlers gazed quietly after him, then slumped up and down their bar, turning very quiet.

Outside, old Withers ran into Dan Miller, who was heading across to the café. "Evenin' young feller," he muttered, his sunken old faded eyes still smoky with anger. "You did a good lick today. The trouble is; it wasn't quite good enough."

Dan halted, gazing up at the taller, older man. "Why wasn't it?" he asked.

"Because Grat'll try his damndest to kill you now, boy, that's why. You never should've done it with your hands. *You should've shot him dead!*" The old man glowered, his chin thrust out, his weathered old face savage. "And you shouldn't have larruped Matt James either. You should've also laid him out stiff. If one don't get you, Deputy, the other one will. Good night!"

Dan stood for a moment watching old Withers stalk across towards his saddle animal tied at the rack in front of the general store. He waited until the old man was astride, riding down the roadway on his way out of town, then Dan also crossed over to that hitchrack. But he didn't halt there; he went on inside.

Evelyn saw him instantly from over near a table where she was working on some ledgers. She closed the large books, glanced at the wall-clock, told the other clerk in the place, an elderly man who wore lavender sleeve garters, she was leaving, and, taking down her shawl from a wall-peg, walked over to the door where Dan was waiting. Without even wishing him a good evening, or even smiling, she hooked her arm over his and led him away.

He helped her hold their unpleasant silence until she turned into the roadway, down which she lived, then he drew up to a halt. "All right," he told her. "Get it off your chest."

She had evidently been simmering for a long while, for she turned on him swiftly saying, "Are you *trying* to get yourself killed!"

"It looks that way, I reckon," he replied. "But after last night I want to live pretty bad."

"Then why don't you *act* like you do. What did you think you'd accomplish out there in the roadway this evening, beating Grat Younger before the whole town and half the digger-pine men?"

"The same thing I tried to accomplish the night I knocked Matt James out, Evelyn."

"You are deliberately trying to get both factions to turn on *you,* instead of each other, Dan."

"No; not exactly," he murmured. "But now that you mention it, that might turn the trick. What I'm tryin' to do is instil enough uncertainty in both sides so they'll hold off from any more direct fights for a few days. That'll give me all the time I need. I hope."

"Time for what, Dan?"

"I need two or three murderers and attempted murderers, Evelyn. I have a man locked in my jailhouse right now I reckon can give me some names. As soon as I've walked you home I'm goin' back to sweat those names out of him."

"Names? You mean the man who shot Gray Appleby?"

"He'll do for a starter," Dan replied. "Then I want to know who shot Fred Clampett. There are a few other things I need answers to, also, but I'll settle for those murderers as a starter."

She was standing very erectly looking up into his face. She started to suddenly speak, then caught herself, loosened a little, turned forward and, taking his arm again, started walking on towards her uncle's and aunt's residence, more relaxed and pensive than before. Finally, just outside the front gate, she swung him half around and said, "What ever made you take up this trade as a law-man, Dan?"

He smiled into her eyes. "I didn't know you then. That's about the only answer that makes sense now, Evelyn."

"Would you give it up?"

He shrugged. "I might. But not until Jefferson's cleaned up. An' accordin' to your lights, whether I accomplish that or not, I'll be six feet under pushin' up grass, so it doesn't make a lot of ——"

"Don't talk like that!" she exclaimed, holding his hand in hers very tightly. "Dan; promise me you'll recruit some of the cow-men to help you."

"I wouldn't dare. If I showed up among those settlers with armed cattlemen at my back, all hell would break loose."

"The townsmen then, Dan, but please — *please* — get someone to help you. No man living can bring off what you're trying."

He reached for the latch, opened the gate and eased her through it. "You go on an' fix some supper. If I get a chance I'll drop by later." He didn't smile at her nor kiss her, nor even say goodbye; he simply nodded a trifle curtly, turned and went walking back up towards the main part of town. He wasn't angry, exactly; he didn't try to gauge his reaction specifically, except to feel annoyed with her. Not for her anxiety on his part, but for her almost smothering solicitation over what he was and what he was trying to do. More women have alienated more men by trying to change them, than by any other way.

He was rounding the corner again, catching his first glimpse of the lighted store windows and the lanterns up and down the roadway, when a gun exploded over across the way and somewhat southward. He heard lead tear into wood not more than five feet from him, and dropped like a stone, rolled back around the corner, and palmed his sixgun.

Another slug struck close, ripping a deep gouge out of the plankwalk. He involuntarily flinched, pushed his forty-five out, and when the third shot came, he saw enough of the assassin's muzzleblast to drive a .45 slug straight towards it.

Down in front of the Great Northern Bar several cowboys standing outside idly talking, yelped and hurled themselves through the louvred front doors of the saloon.

Farther along someone slammed up a window and yelled an alarm.

The next gunshot came from farther northward, as though Dan's ambusher had moved swiftly up behind the opposite buildings for a better aim down that sidestreet where Miller was hiding. That time the bullet was too high, but otherwise it had the range and location down pat.

Dan rolled upright and ran across his intersecting narrow roadway, sprang into the alley-way protection over there and flattened. The next gunshot whistled straight eastward down the deserted roadway. The assassin had waited a little too long; Dan was already safely across the way.

He paused back there to push fresh loads into his sixgun, then stealthily crept northward as far as a small, dark runway between two buildings. There, he eased in, tiptoed up as far as the yonder main roadway again, cocked his sixgun, dropped to one knee, and waited.

But the ambusher over yonder had evidently given it up. No more gunshots came. For a long while there wasn't a sound anywhere. Up and down both sides of the roadway men stood breathlessly waiting to make certain the vicious, sudden fight was over, before peeping out of windows and around doors.

Dan remained where he was a long ten minutes. Down by the Great Northern a man gave a hooting cry. It echoed up and down the roadway. Another man called forth from the opposite side of the road. That one had something substantial to say.

"He pulled out! Rid his damned horse out the back alley over here like its tail was on fire."

Dan stood up, flexed his cramped legs and stepped forth. Evidently the unseen man over yonder who'd seen the bushwhacker leaving, had been telling the truth. No bullets came at any rate.

Down at the Great Northern a dozen or so cowmen pushed outside, guns in hand, peering up and down the deserted roadway. Dan saw them and to avoid an accidental shooting yelled at them.

"Get back inside the saloon! Keep out of the road!"

The rangemen retreated swiftly, contenting themselves with crowding up along the louvred doors, peeking out.

Dan went across the road where his would-be assassin had been waiting in hiding. He found two ejected brass casings from a rifle, not a carbine, pocketed them and strolled down the back-alley over there, not really expecting any more trouble, but keyed up to meet it if he should be proven wrong.

He got all the way down to the jailhouse without encountering a single soul. He passed around front, stepped under his jailhouse wooden awning and remained still and silent, there in the gloomy shadows, watching and waiting. Up at the Great Northern two bold or reckless souls eased outside. Across the road at another saloon other men stepped gingerly forth. Dan turned, put up his gun and entered the marshal's office.

In the back-room he could hear the quick, high lift of curious voices. He took his keys, went over, unlocked the door and flung it back so the prisoners could all see him. They at once stopped speaking. He pointed to the man who'd looked so apprehensive during the earlier talks and beckoned to him.

"Outside you," he growled. "The rest of you get back from the door." After he'd eased his prisoner out and was re-locking the cell door, he looked at the remaining digger-pine men sardonically.

"I thought you long-rifle men would be better shots," he stated. "That yellow-livered friend of yours who just tried to bushwhack

178

me couldn't hit the broad side of a barn from the inside."

He drove his captive out into the front office, slammed the intervening door and pointed towards a bench. The settler went diffidently over and sank down. He was as grey in the face as a dead fish. Dan played on that obvious apprehension to the hilt. With one hand on his holstered sixgun, he said, "Mister; I got no times for playin' games. All I want from you is some names. I'm only goin' to ask you for them once. If you lie, I'll bury you so help me."

The frightened settler whispered, "I'll answer, Deputy. I've had enough of this. I never wanted it to go this far anyway. I'll answer plumb truthfully."

"Who shot Fred Clampett?"

The settler rolled his eyes and moistened his lips. "Carl Wheeler," he whispered hoarsely. "The man you shot the other night."

"You positive of that?"

"I swear it, Deputy!"

"And who shot Gray Appleby."

"You got to protect me. You got to give me your word you'll ——"

"You have my word. *Now answer!*"

"Grat Younger!"

CHAPTER FIFTEEN

Dan digested the information he'd extracted from his jailhouse prisoner thoughtfully. Carl Wheeler was dead so Fred Clampett had been avenged. Gray Appleby's murderer had been savagely beaten at Dan's own hands several hours earler, but he was still alive and free. Furthermore, it was dark now, and regardless of how badly Dan wanted to go after Younger, only a fool deliberately handicapped himself, when his life was at stake. He'd wait until morning.

He put the prisoner back into a cell, flung down his keys and guessed at the time. It was perhaps no later than seven, or perhaps eight o'clock. He also speculated upon the identity of the bushwhacker who'd unsuccessfully attempted to murder him; was, in fact, standing by Fred Clampett's desk still speculating about this, when the roadside door opened and Harper Todd walked in.

"How close did he come?" the cowman

asked, without preceding this question by anything at all, as though Dan would instantly know what he was talking about.

Dan knew. "A couple of feet," he answered. "He wasn't a very good shot or he'd have nailed me sure." Dan sat down and motioned for Todd to do the same. "I had an idea those settlers with their long-rifles would be expert marksmen."

Todd sat. He fished around inside his vest for a cigar, bit off the end, lit up and gazed over at Dan through the smoke. "Interesting thing," he said in a soft tone which belied the speculative brightness of his stare. "They usually are good shots."

Dan eyed the older man. Something was bothering Harper Todd. The cowman had no reason to come down to the jailhouse and pay a social visit; he and Dan Miller just weren't that close at all. "Well," the deputy drawled, "one of them sure isn't."

"Do you reckon it could've been Grat Younger?"

Dan didn't think so and shook his head. "He wasn't in any shape to hold a rifle, let alone accurately aim one, when they hauled him out of town a couple of hours back, Mister Todd."

"My thoughts exactly," murmured the older man, and blew out a long thin streamer of greyish smoke. "So it had to be someone else. Maybe one of the digger-pine men you ordered out of town tonight."

"Maybe," conceded Dan, eyeing Todd sceptically. "But you don't think so. You think it was someone else, an' you've got an uneasy notion you know who he was. Well; I don't like the smell of that cigar enough to sit here an hour waitin' for you to spill it, Mister Todd, so suppose you just blurt it right out."

Harper Todd drew in another mouthful of smoke and slowly expelled it. He was faintly, sardonically, grinning. "You have a way of antagonizing folks," he murmured quietly. "It's almost as though you don't *want* any friends."

"I don't, Mister Todd, until I'm sure who my friends might be. It's a lot easier settlin' with a man you don't like, than with one you do like. You understand?"

Todd understood. He also went right on smoking his potent stogie. He stretched his legs as though he were settling for a long visit, then he said, "Miller; someone not too familiar with one of those long-barrelled muskets wouldn't be a very good shot, I'd say."

"You'd be right, Mister Todd."

"But suppose this 'someone' had a very

good reason for wanting to use one of those damned old muskets when he killed folks; wouldn't you sort of figure he was doing it to cast suspicion on other long-rifle men?"

"The idea might cross m'mind, yes."

Todd leaned his head back, blew smoke at the overhead ceiling and said, "Deputy; when that bushwhacker was trying to nail you this evening, my rangeboss wasn't in the saloon." He lowered his head and soberly gazed straight at Dan. "He'd been in there drinkin' with the rest of us until about half hour earlier. I didn't even miss him until that commotion started outside."

Dan was mildly surprised at what Harper Todd was insinuating, but he was equally as astonished that the cowman was telling him this. He watched Todd push ash off his stogie and tilt the cigar to consider its sullenly glowing red tip. Todd raised his eyes again, giving Dan a straight glance.

"He came strolling back in when the excitement was over, got a glass of whisky from the barman and fished out a dime to pay for a drink with. He was standing right next to me. When he fished out the dime from a vest pocket he dropped something into the sawdust underfoot. I saw it fall but Matt didn't. I put my foot over the thing and waited until just a few minutes ago to bend down and dig it out of the sawdust." Todd reached into a shirt-pocket, brought something forth and tossed it over to Dan Miller. It was the un-fired bullet to a rifle!

Dan turned the bullet over and over, then dug out one of the expended brass cartridge cases he'd been carrying around with him and compared the two. They matched perfectly. He also dug out the flattened chunk of rifle-lead which had been picked up by Todd from beneath Fred Clampett where the marshal had been bushwhacked. In weight, there was no appreciable difference between the two bullets, the sound one and the un-sound one.

Harper Todd went on smoking and sitting. He watched everything Dan did with quiet interest. Finally, he said, "Deputy; until you showed up, the feud between the cowmen and settlers had been simmering for months. You brought all that to a head. Tonight, after I picked up that bullet Matt dropped I went for a walk through the back roads, trying to forget my own feelings and just for a little while, see this whole thing as it really must be."

Dan pocketed the bullets. "And?" he quietly asked.

"And; some things that've happened lately stuck in my craw. For one thing; that fight out at the Salt Lick today."

"What about it?"

"The digger-pine men had their long-range rifles, but my rangeboss wasn't hurt; just one of my men was winged."

"That could be reasonably explained, Mister Todd."

"Maybe. But how long would you or I have to lie out there and shoot at targets as large as men, exposed and under a brilliant sun, and keep missing the one man whose killing would demoralize his companions?"

Dan didn't answer. Evidently Harper Todd hadn't really expected him to, for he went right on speaking, the scepticism in his voice increasing bit by bit.

"And those riflemen had nothing to fear, Deputy; my riders couldn't get within range with their short-barrelled carbines. And there's more, Deputy; why should Matt James be so openly averse to having a showdown with you; because you knocked him out once when he was really too drunk to put up much of a fight? I don't believe that. I know Matt much better than you do. The only time he'd let a thing like that slide, would be when he was plotting his revenge in another way."

"I see," murmured Dan. "By trying to murder me tonight so that it would appear one of the digger-pine men had done it."

"That's what I came up with, Deputy. But just by themselves these things don't mean much — unless Matt and Grat Younger know each other. I mean, *really* know each other."

What Todd was implying hadn't occurred to Dan Miller. It took a long moment to arrive at some kind of a judgement about this possibility. Then he said, "But why? They're both willing to prolong things, sure; that's how they'll keep drawing gunfighter's wages, but ——"

"But suppose they engineered the cowmen an' the settlers into a real head-on fight. And suppose I was killed and one or two of the head digger-pine men were also killed. Wouldn't it be pretty simple for a couple of professional gunfighters and killers to step in and take over, then divide the country between them? Let me put it this way, Deputy; Gray Appleby was an official of the Association. They used him as an experiment to see what reaction would follow. They almost got their head-on war, but you stepped in and stopped it. If that hadn't happened, Deputy, they'd have had their answer."

Dan was beginning to follow Harper Todd's reasoning, finally, so he softly said,

"Mister Todd; if your guesswork is any good, you're goin' to be next. James tried to eliminate me tonight because evidently I'm the real thorn in their flesh, now, but that didn't pan out, so they may have to bushwhack you to get the cowmen mad enough to get together again, and raid the Roan Mountain countryside."

Todd leaned, dropped his cigar into a cuspidor, straightened back and nodded his head. "Seems likely," he said, "doesn't it?"

Dan restlessly arose and paced his little office. "But it's got to be more than just Matt and Grat. It's got to be that feller Wheeler who was so dead-set on starting the massacre that night I shot him, and it's got to be another two or three. Maybe among your men or over among the ——"

"Not my riders," exclaimed Todd firmly. "There's not a man working for me who hasn't been drawing wages from me for less than three years. I *know* those boys, Deputy. They'd shoot digger-pine men out of hand, but they wouldn't turn against me. Before they'd do that, they'd turn on Matt James. They take his orders, but they don't like him. I've seen that in their looks and actions plenty of times."

"All right," Dan conceded. "It's not your men. But Younger and James couldn't possibly pull this off by themselves."

Todd stood up. "They may have to," he drily said. "Wheeler is dead. He was probably one of their pardners among the settlers, but I know most of those other digger-pine men — even the ones you've got locked up right here in this jailhouse. They'd shoot a cowman on sight if they thought they could get away with it; but they'd draw the line at joining in anything like Younger and James are planning for the simple reason that they'd lose just as much as we'd lose, and whatever else we may think of those people, they aren't stupid."

Dan gazed at Harper Todd for a moment, wondering if perhaps Todd hadn't skirted very close to the truth. The reason he wondered that was because of what had happened this very night. It had been very risky for Matt James to have tried drygulching Dan Miller. If he'd been recognized the whole thing would have collapsed around Matt's shoulders.

"If there'd been someone else," he reasoned aloud, "Matt would have had him try at me tonight. You may be right at that, Mister Todd. You just may be right at that. And if you are, then those two have got to get this war started, and damned soon, otherwise they're going to be the only ones around to lose out."

Todd went across to the roadway door and leaned upon it with his hand lying upon the latch. "Any suggestions?" he asked.

Dad nodded. "Yeah. Fetch in your Association officers to this office tomorrow, Mister Todd, an' I'll have old Grant Withers and maybe one or two more of the digger-pine men who are their leaders here also. I've yet to see the men who find out they're being made fools of who don't get mad about it."

Todd nodded and walked out, closed the door gently after himself and walked off into the night. Dan stood a moment thinking; by all rights he should've been tired. He hadn't had much rest the night before, and he'd had a long day too, but something kept bothering him. Someone, right after the assassination-attempt, had yelled out from across the road that he'd seen the drygulcher ride swiftly down the alleyway out of town. That didn't jibe with the fact that the horses of Harper Todd's men had been tied over in front of the Great Northern Bar, unless. . . . He grabbed up his hat, left the jailhouse heading down towards the liverybarn, and scarcely heeded the noise and sounds of nightly revelry northward, up where Jefferson's saloons and dance-halls were.

The liveryman was sound asleep propped against his runway wall, in a tilted-back chair, when Dan came in and shook him by the shoulder. The old man catapulted out of the chair as though he'd been bitten by a horse. When he saw the deputy U.S. marshal standing there, he swore. He was an old man whose lifetime had obviously been spent in a rough world; he could swear steadily for three minutes without once using the same word twice.

Dan waited for the furious storm to pass, then asked if anyone had hired a horse at dusk or earlier, and had brought it back an hour or so later, having hardly ridden it at all.

"I hadn't ought to tell you," stormed the indignant older man, "creepin' up on folks an' scarin' 'em out o' five years growth like that. I hadn't ought to tell you nothin' at all!"

"I apologize," said Dan, near to smiling at the old man's apoplectic rage. "But it's important."

"All right. Yes; I hired out a horse an' tied it out back o' the barn in the alleyway like I was told. I didn't see him take it away, but after all that shootin' up the road about an hour or such a matter back, I went out into the alley to look aroun', and he'd fetched the critter back. I knew he'd used it 'cause the horse was breathin' hard, even though it hadn't been ridden far, 'cause it warn't even sweatin'. Now are you satisfied — fingerin' folks in the middle o' the night until you might' near scairt 'em into a stroke. How'd I know you wasn't some bloody-hand on the warpath come to hoist my hair?"

"Oldtimer," soothed Dan, "there haven't been any hostile redskins around here for ____"

"You don't have to tell me what there is an' what there ain't in Idaho Territory, Deputy; I was trailin' bloody-hands when you were soakin' the slats o' your cradle!"

"Well; I apologize again, oldtimer. But like I said it's downright important to ____"

"An' furthermore if you don't let Al Dugan out'n that jailhouse up yonder, you're goin' to have my death on your hands. I'm an old man; I can't do this hard work no longer. On top o' that I got a weak heart; I could keel over from exertion any second. It'd all be on your conscience, Deputy-hmph! — sneakin' up on folks in the middle o' the night!"

Dan waited again for the storm to pass, then he said, "If I let Dugan out will you

191

tell me the name of the man who used that horse?"

"You bet I will! His name was Matt James!"

CHAPTER SIXTEEN

If Matt had been successful, no one would probably ever have asked the liveryman that question, because the one man who would've been particularly interested would have been dead, and the only other man who might, in time, have been interested — Harper Todd — would have been slated for early execution also.

But Matt had failed, and now Dan Miller knew who had tried to kill him, as well as how clever Matt had been at it, hiring a horse and afterwards riding hard down the alley southward to give the impression he was a digger-pine settler on his way out of town after an unsuccessful assassination attempt.

It was clever, Dan conceded that, and when, the following morning, Doctor Lawrence met Dan at the café eating breakfast and told him Fred Clampett was making a remarkable recovery, Dan afterwards sauntered up and paid Marshal Clampett a visit.

Fred was full of questions; he'd heard of the fight out at the Salt Lick. He'd also heard the gunfire in the roadway the night before. Dan had a lot of explaining to do, but when he unburdened himself on what he and Harper Todd thought might be in the making, Fred Clampett was dumb-founded.

Trouble he had more or less been expecting for some time before he'd been shot, but simple trouble, not the complicated, mixed-up, devious kind of trouble Dan talked of to him. He sat up in bed and probed Dan for every scrap of information the deputy had, then he lay back staring at the ceiling, quiet for a long while, before turning his head on the pillow and saying, "They'd have to be meeting, if any of this is true, Dan. With all the watchers out now, they couldn't meet together very easily without being spotted. An' that would arouse questions; Matt's supposed to be the bitterest enemy of Grat, and also, Grat's supposed to hate Matt's guts."

Dan nodded in agreement, but he wasn't too concerned with where, or even whether, James and Younger secretly met. He had in mind striking straight to the core of all this by going after Younger. Not especially because Grat was part of a secret plot, but because of what his prisoner down at the jailhouse had told him: Grat Younger was the gunman who had killed Gray Appleby. Still and all, though, he liked Fred Clampett, so he sat there killing another hour before he found a way to get outside again. Even then, Marshal Clampett wasn't ready to abandon all thought of participating some way in the coming storm.

Doc Lawrence was outside on his little porch, feet propped up, smoking a pipe and reading a newspaper. Dan said, "Doctor; you better keep a close watch on him. He thinks he's ready to jump out of bed and go culling wildcats."

The physician nodded with no great show of concern. "The minute he swung his legs over and hit the floor, Deputy, he'd faint. I won't have to keep a very close watch; Mother Nature'll do that for me."

Dan went down to his jailhouse, listened to the growls and outcries of his hungry prisoners, took Alf Dugan out of a cell obstensibly to help him haul back trays of food for the others, then he made Dugan sit down in the outer office while he told him he'd release Dugan on two conditions.

"One is that you'll get a horse right away, ride up to Grant Withers claim, tell the old man to round up the other former spokes-men for the digger-pine men and fetch them down here to my office immediately. The other condition, Dugan, is that you pass me your word you'll not take any further hand in this feudin' no matter what anyone says — including Grat Younger."

Dugan solemnly raised his right hand as though speaking under oath, rolled his eyes around, and nodded his head vigorously up and down. "You got m'solemn word," he intoned. "My plumb solemn word, Deputy."

"Then get out of here and get up there to Withers's cabin."

Dugan left in an ungainly lope. Dan watched him heading straight for the livery-barn. When he turned to step back inside his office Evelyn Benson was standing there on the northward plankwalk watching him.

"I don't see anything to smile about," she said. "Dan; I didn't mean to be bossy last night, or demanding. It's simply that I was worried and frightened."

He stepped back for her to precede him inside, then he kicked the door closed. "I was worried and scairt too," he told her, still looking slightly amused, "about twenty minutes after I left you last night."

"I know. I heard the shooting and went out to find out what was happening. I thought you might be involved."

"It wasn't my idea," he said, and smiled at her.

"Were you hurt?"

"Only my pride," he murmured. "Now you better get on back to the store, Evelyn. I've got visitors coming. It'd be better if you weren't here when they arrived." He opened the door for her.

She went over to him, raised both hands and placed them gently against him, leaned forward and brushed his mouth with her lips. "I'll be waiting for you to walk me home tonight," she murmured, and departed. As he'd done with Alf Dugan, Dan stood in his office doorway gazing up the sunlighted hot roadway watching her walk away. She was a strikingly handsome woman from any direction.

He made a smoke, thumbed back his hat, cocked up his chair in front of Fred Clampett's desk and composed himself for the waiting he had to do. At best, the diggerpine men couldn't reach town for another two hours or thereabouts, even though he was satisfied Harper Todd and the Association cowmen would ride in much sooner. He wasn't too concerned, until, with his smoke half consumed, a Todd rangerider came sliding to a flinging halt outside at the jailhouse hitchrack and sprinted up to burst inside the office in breathless haste, wet with sweat and red in the face. Dan's feet came down with a crash; without being told he knew something serious had happened, and also without anything more than the look on that rider's face, he thought he knew what it was. The cowboy blurted out his words.

"Harper Todd's been shot!"

Dan uncoiled up out of his chair. "Dead?"

The cowboy shrugged. "Wasn't when I headed for town, but he sure didn't look very good either."

"Where is he?"

"At the ranch. Matt and the other fellers are with him."

"Matt? . . . Matt James is with him?"

"Yeah."

"Wait until I get my horse," ordered Dan, swinging past out towards the plankwalk. He made a dash for the liverybarn, didn't even bother to look for the liveryman, who wasn't in sight, but got his own horse rigged out, sprang aboard and rode out of the barn northward. The rangeman was waiting for him up there. The two of them left town in a careening rush which scattered roadway traffic and caused some articulate indignation to float after, in their wake.

Dan didn't slow for nearly a long mile after they were well away from town, and even then he simply exchanged a fast run for a quick gallop as he questioned the cowboy.

"Where did Todd get shot?"

The cowboy didn't know, exactly. "Out on the range somewhere; him an' Matt was bringing in some horses. He'd maybe have died too, 'cepting some of the other fellers was out that way too, heard the shot, and came bustin' it over a hill an' down to where Matt was kneeling beside Mister Todd."

Dan looked at the cowboy as he muttered, "You got no idea how right you are." Then he said, "What did Matt do?"

The cowboy looked baffled. "Do? Why, he rode in with the others to fetch out the wagon and haul Mister Todd to the ranch."

"Did he send you to town?"

"No. I left as soon as I heard what'd happened. I hollered at Doc Lawrence who was sitting up there on his front porch, then I rode on down an' got you."

"Doc leave?" Dan asked, and the cowboy shrugged, saying he hadn't actually seen the physican ride out of town but he was certain he had. Dan's next question was more to the point of what was in his mind. "Did you see the wound; how bad was it?"

"I didn't see it, Deputy. I left the ranch as soon as I could."

There was nothing more to be gained from the rangerider, so Dan concentrated on steadily riding until he could make out the Todd-ranch buildings up ahead where hot sunlight and beckoning tree-shade cast their alternating shadows of light and dark. By then, however, the cowboy's initial shock and excitement had passed; he was turning grim and vengeful. He said, "They never should've done it to Mister Todd, Deputy. They're goin' to wish to gawd they'd never done that!"

Dan slowed again. They were approaching the buildings; there was no longer any need for speed. He turned, gazed at the stormy face of his companion and said, "If you mean the digger-pine men, an' if you're figurin' they shot Harper Todd, you're wrong."

The rangerider was astonished. "Wrong? How can I be wrong, for gosh sakes? Who else'd slip aroun' an' bushwhack cowmen? Look what they done to Gray Appleby. Deputy; you don't know what you're ——"

"I'm not wrong," broke in Dan, reining over towards the main house where two rangemen were caring for a lathered horse at the tie-rack. "I know exactly what I'm sayin', too, mister; the digger-pine settlers

200

didn't shoot Harper Todd!"

Dan reined up, stepped down and flung his leathers around the hitchrack. He shot the pair of nearby cowboys a look. "He still alive?" Dan asked. The cowboys glumly nodded and kept silent. They looked equally as forbidding as the man who'd accompanied Dan from town.

The front door was ajar so Dan walked on in. There was another dark-faced cowboy in the parlour. He dourly nodded and went right on building the smoke he was rolling. Dan could hear familiar voices so he went through the house until he came to the darkened room where Harper Todd lay limply. Doctor Lawrence hadn't arrived at the ranch more than five or ten minutes ahead of the deputy U.S. marshal, but he was already grimly and deftly at work.

Matt James looked up as Dan entered, then looked back at the grey, lifeless features upon the pillow again. Matt's own features were smoothed out in an expression of total impassivity.

Dan tiptoed over and gazed downward. The bullet which had struck Harper Todd had come from close up. That didn't surprise Dan at all; in fact it confirmed his secret suspicions. The bullet had pierced Todd from behind, and that didn't surprise

Dan either. What did surprise him, though, was that after Doc Lawrence got the shirt and soggy underwear cut away and the bullet hole wiped clean, it was evident that the slug had been deflected by bone, perhaps Todd's shoulderblade or collarbone, and instead of ploughing straight on through to kill Todd, had angled predictably upwards, ripping out a jagged piece of living flesh, up and over the shoulder.

Doc Lawrence gazed up at Dan and said, "Another one; he's lost a lot of blood. I can't tell yet how much, but I'd say not as much as Fred Clampett lost, which means, unless he's got a weak heart or unless complications set in, he'll pull through. But it'll be a long time. Maybe it'll be a year before he can use his left hand and arm again."

Dan looked over at the rangeboss. Matt wasn't looking at Dan, he was closely watching Doc Lawrence work. Dan said, "Matt; how did it happen?"

James mumbled when he answered, and never once looked at the lawman. "We was after some horses. A fresh remuda we needed on the ranch. We were split up — maybe twenty yards apart, more or less — when someone fired at him from a gully."

Doctor Lawrence said, "He must've been

sitting his horse on the very edge of that gully, James. This bullet didn't travel very far before it hit him."

"Yeah," agreed the rangeboss. "He was sittin' up there lookin' down. Maybe he'd seen the bushwhacker, I don't know. I was anglin' away northward, when the gunshot sounded. I looked around and he was falling."

Dan said, "Didn't you see anyone?"

Matt nodded. "I saw him all right, but he went down that gully a hundred yards as tight as he could ride before I did, an' then I was more worried about Todd, so I didn't get a shot at him until he was out of carbine range."

"Which way did he go?"

Finally, Matt James raised his grey eyes to Dan's face. "Straight over towards Roan Mountain," he replied, enunciating very clearly, leaving no doubt in anyone's mind what he meant by that statement.

Dan asked no more questions and a moment or two later Matt James tiptoed out of the room on an errand for the doctor. Dan bent down and swiftly said, "Doc; when will he regain consciousness? Keep your voice down!"

The physician paused at his work and raised puzzled eyes to Dan's face. "Maybe an hour," he whispered. "Maybe not for six or eight hours. Why? What's the mystery?"

Dan said in the same low, intense tone of voice. "The man who shot him just walked out of this room to get you more hot water and clean rags."

Doctor Lawrence stiffened. His eyes flew wide open. He swung to glance over at the doorway, then swung back again. "Do you know what you're talking about?" he hissed.

"You can bet your money I know what I'm talkin' about, Doc. An' you can also bet your money that the minute you and I leave this ranch, and Matt James can send the rangeriders so far out they won't be able to hear another gunshot, Harper Todd's going to die right here, without ever being able to say a word!"

Doctor Lawrence straightened up staring at Dan. He started to speak, checked himself, then started over again. 'I'll be through here in a half hour," he said swiftly. "You stay with him. I'll go back to town and get several men who can be trusted and send them right back. All right, Deputy?"

"All wrong," growled Dan. "You and I're goin' back to town together, an' we're goin' to take Harper Todd back with us in his own wagon, so you make those bandages real good. I'll go see that the wagon is ready."

As Dan strode out of the room, Matt James re-entered it.

CHAPTER SEVENTEEN

Getting the wagon ready to take Harper Todd to Jefferson was no problem; three of the ranch-hands even helped Dan Miller put the harness on a fresh team, and afterwards, when he rode across the yard towards the house, those three men, at Dan's invitation, saddled their horses and went across the yard with him.

Dan anticipated some resistance from James, but it didn't materialize. It might have, Dan thought, for when he entered the house to have the unconscious man carried out to the wagon by those three riders, Matt, who had known nothing of any of this until that moment, said he thought they should leave Todd where he was; that he was afraid the bumping along in the wagon might kill him. Doctor Lawrence squelched that in the only way it could've been authoritatively done: By giving his professional opinion that no such danger existed. Matt was left standing. Dan had out-thought him and Doc Lawrence had out-manoeuvred him.

As those three rangemen picked up their employer very carefully and took him out to the wagon Dan said, "Matt; maybe you'd better come along."

James looked quizzically at the lawman. "Why?"

Dan shrugged. "Who knows what can happen between here and Jefferson. Suppose some digger-pine men are watching the ranch right now. They'll realize Todd's not dead."

Matt nodded. "Yeah; they might make another try," he said.

They left some of the Todd-ranch crew back at the home-place. There were the three riders Dan had recruited, Matt James, Doc and Dan. Dan and Doctor Lawrence drove up atop the wagon-box with their horses tied to the tailgate following along. Nothing much was said for a long while, or until Matt pointed southward as they came into the outskirts of town, and commented that those distant men riding all in a group far down there, looked to him like digger-pine men.

Dan looked and privately agreed that's what they looked like, but he passed it all off easily by saying they were probably coming to town for flour or sugar, but that whatever they wanted, there'd be no trouble in his town because he wouldn't stand for it.

They lost sight of the settlers when Doc steered the wagon around behind his combination office and residence, looped the lines and jumped down to go open a back door. He then beckoned for the dismounting rangeriders to fetch Harper Todd inside, which they proceeded to do.

Dan lingered a while, waiting to catch Doc Lawrence alone. When he eventually did that, in the room across the hall where Fred Clampett blissfully slept through all this, he whispered to Doc not to leave Todd alone with Matt James for a single moment. He also said he had to briefly leave, go down to his office and talk to some settlers.

Doc Lawrence was uneasy. "I'm no gunfighter," he protested. "I never even was a very good free-for-all fist-fighter, Deputy. What am I supposed to do?"

"Just keep those three rangemen in there with you. They're loyal to Todd. They wouldn't let Matt do anything. And you stay with him too."

"Listen, Deputy; why don't you arrest James and take him out of here with you?"

208

"I couldn't hold him five minutes. I've got to have better proof than I've got. In other words, Doc, I need Harper Todd to wake up and point a finger at James."

"But are you confident that when he wakes up he will do that?"

"I'm stakin' a lot on my convictions about that, Doc. Now I've got to go, but as soon as I possibly can, I'll be back. You do your part an' maybe — just maybe — we'll be able to end all the feuding before this day's over."

The physician accompanied Dan to his front door and watched him walk out into the hot, bright sunshine, heading for the marshal's office down the dusty roadway.

Seven men were lounging outside the building, waiting, when he walked up. Only one of them nodded: Grant Withers. The other digger-pine men leaned in the hot shade, waiting; saying nothing, sceptical of both Dan Miller and his purpose for having them here in town, and waiting for this scepticism to be substantiated in whatever Dan did next, or not, as the case should turn out to be.

Even old Withers had the craggy, hard look of a man with an unfavourable judgement balanced in his mind when Dan opened the office door, jerked his head and looked at the old man, waiting for him to walk past.

They entered the office and Dan stepped over in front of the door, leaning upon it as he closed it. "I'll get right to the point," he said. "I called this meeting because I want you men to align yourselves with the law. Grat Younger is a murderer and I'm going to get him, directly, and lock him up. When he's no longer giving the orders among your people, I want you men to move right in where he left off, and keep any hotheads among your folks from starting this thing all over again."

"What about Matt James?" growled a burly, dark man, looking more sceptical of Dan than ever.

"Matt James will be dead or locked up, too, by sundown."

Grant Withers stood, saying nothing. Another of his companions said, "Deputy; I'm for stoppin' the feudin'. Ain't no real point to it no-how. Regardless of how that there survey line was drawn crooked the first time, it's drawn right now, and both sides got plenty o' salt. I been askin' my neighbours for nigh a month now — what's the fightin' about?"

Dan let this man finish then quietly told them Harper Todd had been shot down. He followed this up with his and Harper Todd's theory of how two gunfighters were deliberately trying to provoke a real battle which would decimate both sides, and finally, he told them he wanted them to go back up to their people and keep them out of the way by whatever ruse they had to use, until Dan could locate and arrest Grat Younger.

Old Grant Withers shook his head at the deputy U.S. lawman. "Too late for anythin' like that," he said. "His spies saw the lot o' us headin' down here to town, Mister Miller. By now I reckon he's got his chosen hatchet-men on their way down here too."

"What hatchet-men?" Dan demanded.

"He's got a couple of young fellers who're just beginnin' to rut a little. He's been workin' on them for quite a spell now, shaping them up to fight for him. He's done a right good job of it, Mister Miller. They don't even carry their rifles any more — just sixguns. Lashed down sixguns with the front sights filed off; genuine gunfighters, Mister Miller, an' my guess is that they're somewhere around town, or skulkin' out yonder waitin' for us fellers to leave town so's they can jump us an' make us tell what we were doin' here, all in a group."

Dan thought a moment, then said, "You reckon Younger'll be with 'em?"

211

Several of the men nodded but only old Withers spoke up. "He'll be with 'em, Deputy. He needs them boys to protect his back now."

Dan was quietly thoughtful for as long as it took him to manufacture a smoke and light it. Then he said, "You boys stay right here inside this office. If you hear shootin' directly, you still stay right here in this office. You understand?"

No one said he understood and no one nodded his head to indicate he would obey, but as Dan took down a carbine from the wall-rack one of the digger-pine men held out his long-barrel rifle. "Do a sight better job with one of these," he said. Dan shook his head; he wasn't used to such a weapon. He thanked the settler, then left the marshal's office, stepped around back and went down the southward alleyway towards the lower environs of Jefferson.

He passed the blacksmith shop, the saddle and harness store and the buggy works — where someone was whistling an old marching song lustily — and was approaching the liverybarn when he saw a man angling into town from the southwest, with a long-rifle balanced across his lap. He was on the verge of moving on past; he wasn't looking for trouble with just any digger-pine man;

besides, the men up in his office had declared the pair of recruits Grat Younger had been training didn't carry rifles any longer. Without any warning whatsoever that settler raised his rifle, took brief aim and fired at Dan Miller. He'd recognized the deputy, of course, and as a man from up around Roan Mountain he'd been hostile; at the least he'd be antagonistic, but Dan was astonished at the savagery of that brief glimpse he and the settler had of each other, when the man tried to kill him. It didn't occur to Dan until the whistling man back at the buggy works let off a startled yelp and stopped his whistling, that someone had made a bad mistake; maybe Younger's recruits didn't *ordinarily* carry their long-rifles, but this time they were carrying them, because, no sooner had that man out there fired and barely missed, and Dan hit the ground, a second rifle let fly, and that one would have drilled Dan dead-centre if he'd been still standing upright. But that second marksman hadn't been firing from the saddle either. Dan saw him by craning around. He was standing on the off side of his horse using the saddle-seat as his musket-rest.

Suddenly, there was that selfsame quick, breathless hush hanging over the town which had accompanied that other gunfight Dan had been involved in when a different killer had made an earlier attempt upon Dan's life. The whistler at the buggy works was silent. At the liverybarn there was neither a sound nor a sighting; whoever was inside that building was discreetly remaining hidden. Everywhere, up and down the roadway, it was the same. As though by magic, Dan Miller was entirely alone.

He had a serious problem, too. Although he could see both his enemies out there on the range below town, he couldn't shoot either one of them. They could pepper away at him all day, and unless he got to safety, they'd eventually cut him down, but he couldn't hurt them. They had long-barrel rifles, he had a short-barrel Winchester carbine.

He got up and sprinted over into the liverybarn. One of his enemies fired but the other one turned his horse to ride in closer, and that was exactly what Dan had hoped for. They were sufficiently bent on destroying him to push too hard, become too reckless.

The elfish liveryman popped his head out the harness-room door frantically gesturing. "Get out'n here," he hissed at Dan. "Don't turn my barn into no battleground, consarn it, Deepity. I got horses in here could get shot accidental-like. Who's goin' to pay for the damage?"

Dan raised his carbine. The liveryman looked, squawked, and tumbled backwards out of sight. Dan was lowering the weapon when in the yonder roadway a man's cruel laughter burst out. He recognized the voice instantly: Grat Younger! Right then it hit Dan hard: Those two digger-pine gunmen out southward had deliberately baited him, forcing him to keep his eyes on them while Younger slipped into town and got behind him. He was sealed off and bottled up! They had him covered from behind and in front; the second he left the liverybarn by either doorway, they'd riddle him.

"Hey, lawman," Younger called from some unseen vantage point out front beyond Dan's sight, "you walked right into it. You're a dead turkey any way you look at it. I owe you this. No man does what you did to Grat Younger and walks away alive. Them two squatters out there got you out-gunned too, Deputy. If you try grabbin' a horse and makin' a run for it over the range, they'll string out your innards for a hundred yards. You come out front an' I'll do the same with my sixgun." Younger paused, then laughed again. He was thoroughly enjoying himself now.

The liveryman poked his elfish head out the harness-room door and bleated again. "Deepity! Get out'n here. You're goin' to get me an' my —"

"Be glad to," Dan exclaimed. "Just tell me how!"

"The back alley, consarn it, or over through that door yonder between them stalls. It leads next door into the forge-room o' the buggy works. Cut that danged door there myself years back when they used to do my shoein' an' fittin' for me."

Dan looked around, located the door, and ran towards it. He knew what the buggy works looked like; he'd been there before. It was a large, sooty place where wagons, buggies, even freight outfits, were manufactured. In many ways it resembled a blacksmith's shop, in other ways a shipyard on a miniature scale, or a carpentry shop complete with all the shavings and tools and benches. He entered the place, saw two round-eyed men flattened against the northward wall, and eased that conveniently intervening door at his back, softly closed. One of the workers over against the far wall screwed up his face in desperate pantomime and pointed out through the sunlighted, dead-silent doorway yonder into the equally as hushed and golden roadway. Dan nodded; he already knew about where Younger was, from hearing him speak a while back. He began working his way around the grimy walls towards that roadside doorway.

From southward, out beyond town, a youthful voice sang out. Dan paused for the answer but it never came. Evidently one of Younger's recruits back out there wanted to know where their entrapped enemy was. Just as evidently, Younger was wondering the same thing, but was not going to risk disclosure by yelling back.

Dan got over next to the doorway, wiped sweat off the palm of his gun-hand and took back several big breaths. He could see across the empty roadway, and somewhat to his left, on up the roadway, but he couldn't see southward at all without leaning his head out. The town was as silent as though it were abandoned. That brilliant sunshine was everywhere; its heat was rolling up over the town in lemon-yellow layers.

Dan tried to imagine where Younger would be crouched, waiting. There were a dozen places for a bushwhacker to be, in that dazzling brightness and total silence. Dan looked at his cocked gun; he looked back where the petrified workmen were breathlessly watching from their grimy wall. He faced the deadly roadway one last time. There was nothing left for him to do except walk out there and hunt Younger down. Otherwise he'd have to cringe in the sooty gloom of the harness shop, with the whole town changing its mind about him.

CHAPTER EIGHTEEN

He eased forward for a peek, saw nothing and eased back again. One of the workmen hissed and frantically waved towards the back-alley. He had seen something move out there, to the south, and kept gesticulating about this. Dan nodded, eased back and spun around, making his silent way back across towards the other large opening in the smoky old room.

He dropped low, looked out, saw the youthful gunman stalking towards the liverybarn's alley-way exit from the west, pushed out his gun and softly called. The digger-pine man whipped straight up, caught off-guard, and swung his gun. Dan fired. The settler dropped his weapon, bent far over and fell head-first.

Out front, someone fired two random shots into the liverybarn runway. Dan heard them both strike wood as he sprang up and ran back towards the front of the buggy works again. He saw dirty gunsmoke rising above a recessed doorway across the road, and northward, where an old wooden awning kept out the sunlight.

He knew where Younger was at last. He also knew something else; evidently Grat didn't know about that connecting doorway leading from the liverybarn into the buggy works, because Grat was still concentrating his whole attention upon the liverybarn.

Dan weighed his chances and made his decision. He'd have the greater part of two or three seconds, once he stepped outside, to get Younger before Grat recovered from his surprise that Dan wasn't at the liverybarn after all, and tried to get Dan.

It wasn't a whole lot of time, but it would be enough, providing Dan could spring far enough northward to see into Grat's recessed doorway. He made one fatal mistake. He was ignoring that other youthful diggerpine gunman south of town. If it was an understandable mistake, it was nevertheless the one mistake no one can afford to make in a gunfight because gunfighters do not get second chances.

Up the northward roadway somewhere, a man's voice sang out. For a moment this invisible caller held Dan's attention, and perhaps held the attention of everyone else in town also, because his voice was the only sound anywhere around; the only voice, in fact, to be raised, since Younger had taunted Dan Miller nearly twenty minutes earlier.

But Dan could neither place where that man called from, nor what he was calling about. At any rate, no one answered him, if they were supposed to. He called one more time, then did not raise his voice again.

The brace of workmen were still standing stiffly over against the back-wall, barely even moving their eyes now. Evidently the terrific tension had gotten to them, turning both of them rigid with apprehension. Dan eyed them, eyed the back-alley entrance to the shop, turned and ran a long, slow look outward where the sunshine mercilessly burned downward.

He left the carbine behind, sprang out, and the second he felt that fierce summertime heat across his shoulders he sprinted northward, all the time keeping both his face and his gun turned towards that yonder recessed doorway where Grat Younger was crouched, waiting him out.

He was almost there; almost up to where he'd have his sighting of Younger, when the rifle slammed its sharp, biting sound through layers of heavy heat, echoing and re-echoing up through the full length and breadth of town.

Dan didn't feel the ball strike him, exactly; at least he had no immediate sensation of pain, but instead he felt as though someone had struck him violently across the back with a huge paddle. His breath momentarily left him. The impact made him nearly fall. He had to instinctively push out both arms to avoid reeling into a store-front. He knew he'd been hit; he also knew that by all the rules of the gunfighter's game he should be dead, for he'd made the one inexcusable mistake: He'd concentrated so hard on getting one man that he'd all but entirely neglected a deadly enemy who'd been somewhere behind him.

But he was still upright, able to co-ordinate his movements and think sharply, after that first breathless shock passed, so he pushed inward around a curving store-front where he should've been able to see Grat Younger, and Grat saw Dan, simultaneously with Dan's own vision of Younger.

Grat fired first. Dan's reflexes had been the slightest bit impaired. But Grat had been tense so long, had been sweating Dan out so, that his own reflexes were jerky and raw. He missed and broke a glass window on Dan's right side. The glass made a pleasant tinkling sound as it fell around Miller's feet.

Grat was pressing back into his doorway. Dan fired, holding his sixgun low. He thumbed back the dog and simultaneously depressed the trigger. His second shot, for some reason, sounded even louder than his first shot. Grat dropped to one knee, raised his sixgun, hesitated long enough to shake his head, and fired low. The bullet cut through Dan's trouser leg low and on the inside, searing across the muscles of his left leg two inches above his boot-top. That wound hurt instantly and fiercely, but it wasn't serious at all. The pain made Dan's next shot wild. It struck the door panelling behind and above Younger splintering wood. Younger sagged away as though flinching and raised his left arm, bent it and laid his sixgun across the crooked forearm. He held that position for what to Dan seemed a whole lifetime without firing, then tipped down his gun-barrel, wilted from the head down, and fell forward out across the plank-walk with one hand dangling in the manured dust of the roadway, the other hand gently opening to allow his cocked sixgun to lie loosely in the hot brilliance of the sunshine. Grat Younger was dead.

Dan drew in a shallow breath. It was

beginning to pain him to breathe. He waited a full ten seconds, watching Younger, before he re-loaded and hung the sixgun back into its hip-holster. He knew that digger-pine man who'd shot him was out there somewhere, probably trying to skulk up behind him. He also knew that as long as he remained where he was with his back to a solid plank wall, that digger-pine rifleman was going to sooner or later have to face him, if he meant to persist in his attempt to kill Miller.

Finally, he knew one more thing. He was hard hit. Unless that rifleman came soon, Dan Miller was going to pass out, and when that happened, he'd be a sitting duck for that rifleman.

Up the road, somewhere in the vicinity of the Great Northern Bar that same voice which had called out earlier, called out again, but as before, the words were indistinguishable to Miller in his shadowy place amid the broken glass and widening red stain from his own blood. The man called out commandingly twice, then went silent again. It sounded to Dan as though someone up there was trying to take a hand in this private fight. He had no idea who that might be up there, and didn't actually try very hard to guess who he was. It was beginning to be necessary for him to exert an effort to keep his eyes open. He was, for some reason he didn't try to fathom, getting sleepy.

A rifle exploded slightly southward and across the road. Dan's alertness returned with a rush. That, he knew, had to be the digger-pine man who'd shot him earlier. He guessed that the rifleman had seen dead Grat Younger and was trying to get up northward over there, far enough to also get a sighting at Dan. Why he'd prematurely fired a round, Dan had no idea until another rifle fired back from farther uptown. That, Dan told himself, had to be either old Grant Withers or one of the settlers he'd left at the jailhouse.

Again the rifleman across the road let fly, evidently duelling with that other gunman up the road. Dan wiped sweat off his face and decided that as long as someone was diverting his enemy, he'd try an ambush of his own. He knelt down heavily, checked his sixgun and, bracing his body with his left hand, leaned forward to see out. At that same moment his enemy across the road and southward also exposed him, but like Dan had mistakenly done earlier, the digger-pine man was concentrating upon his other enemy farther up the roadway. For Dan that oversight had proven *nearly* fatal, for his foe-man it proved *definitely* fatal. Dan fired his sixgun simultaneously with the digger-pine gunman's gunshot. The rifleman let off a high cry, sprang out of his hiding place and hit the ground hard, then rolled into plain sight, dead and face up in the bitter lemon sunlight.

Dan let all his breath out, pushed back upright and supported himself upon the bullet-scarred, surrounding store-front wall. The drowsiness was returning again, but more persistently now. Some instinctive warning told him to remain where he was, but an urge to get away from this place motivated him to step out into the sunlight. He looked up and down the empty roadway. For five seconds nothing happened, then that insistent voice up somewhere in the vicinity of the Great Northern saloon called down a quick, flat warning to Dan. Through the quickening sharpness of his struggling alertness he finally knew whose voice that was: U.S. Marshal Fred Clampett!

He turned slightly and started moving towards Clampett. He didn't see him but he knew Fred would be somewhere up there across the road from the saloon; perhaps on the porch of Doctor Lawrence's cottage, or possibly pressing flat just below a window sill up there. It didn't occur to him to wonder about Marshal Clampett using a rifle instead of his carbine and sixgun. In fact it didn't even occur to him that he was now in more deadly peril than ever before, until just before the gunshot came. Then, it was too late.

He was too fuzzy in the mind, too unsteady in the body, and finally, he was too confused in the instincts which might otherwise have warned him, to remember that Grat Younger was far from being his only enemy.

He heard the sixgun roar, but it sounded a very long way off. Then the ground jumped up and hit him hard in the chest jarring him just for a flaring second back to total rationality.

Matt James! He'd completely forgotten Matt James! He stopped trying to raise up and instead threw himself sideways. When the next bullet struck where he had been, it roiled up a small burst of dust and dirt, showering him with both. But he'd seen James; the gunfighter walked out into plain sight from beside the Great Northern Bar, took a wide-legged stance and raised his sixgun for the final shot.

Dan fired first. James hesitated a moment, looking with surprise over the tip of his sixgun barrel. Dan drew back his sixgun-hammer with an instinctive reflex in that precious moment which was the sere, blinding second in all Time, when of two men, only one could seize the initiative and survive. Dan fired again.

That time James braced hard. The slug had hit him. Matt's long face lost its wilful ferocity slowly; it assumed an expression of almost gentle softness. He squeezed his trigger. The bullet hit a post three feet high behind Dan, over near a store-front. Matt let his breath out slowly and re-cocked his gun.

The rifle sounded with its high, sharply positive sound over across the northward roadway. James turned half way, swinging his gun in this fresh direction. Another gun erupted, this time a carbine, from the doorway of the general store. James still didn't go down, but his reaction was signal; he began to weave. From the open doorway of the jailhouse a fusillade of rifle shots crashed and thundered. Matt James was literally torn loose from the sidewalk and bodily hurled up against the corner of the saloon's wall. He fell like a broken rag doll.

Dan raised up. He saw Fred Clampett begin to stand up from behind the palings of Doctor Lawrence's front porch. He also saw those lanky, stony-faced settlers, led by grim old Grant Withers, boil out of his jail-house office to go striding away in two separate directions, northward and south-ward, to examine the dead gunmen. Finally, he saw Evelyn Benson stop past the doorway of the store, lean a carbine upon the front wall, and start down toward him.

He smiled. She was running. Farther back Doctor Lawrence was also loping down towards him. But the first man to reach him was old Grant Withers. He had four of his leathery-faced, bleak-eyed digger-pine neighbours with him. They gently knelt and leaned there, holding to their long-barrel guns and studying his injuries.

Old Withers drawled in his quiet tone: "Lie easy, Deputy. You got one on the inside o' your laig. You got another one just under your shoulder. We seen the dog give you that one — from behind — an' you also leaked a mite o' blood. Just lie easy, the sawbones is comin'."

Dan blinked back the drowsiness. "Younger dead?" he husked.

Withers nodded. "Deader'n stone, Deputy."

"And — Matt James?"

Withers nodded again in the same solemn way. "Likewise," he murmured. "Two more down yonder too — fellers from up aroun' Roan Mountain, Deputy — but if you hadn't got 'em we would've. Them kind we got no use for."

Evelyn came up and got down on both knees beside him in the fierce, hot sunlight, while he was still gazing straight at old Withers. "One thing more, Grant," he whispered, letting Evelyn cradle his head in her lap. "Before I die I want you to pass me your word about something."

Withers leaned down, softly smiling. "You're not goin' to die, son. Be laid up a spell, but with a pretty nurse — shucks — you'll be better off'n all the rest of us. An' about what you're goin' to ask — we already know. You got our word on it, too. From this day forward — no more feudin'. The cowmen can lay claim to whatever part o' that lousy Salt Lick they want. No more fightin', Deputy. No more killin'. All the salt in the world ain't worth it. We pass you our words on that."

Old Withers picked up Dan's hand, held it a moment, and put it gently down again and raised his eyes as Doctor Lawrence came up, panting hard, and knelt quickly. Withers said, "Miss Evelyn; he's plumb unconscious. You reckon he heard what I just told him?"

Evelyn's smoky eyes were dry-hot and unusually bright. "If he didn't, Mister Withers," she said unsteadily, "I'll be right there when he comes around. I'll tell him."

Old Withers smiled at the lovely girl and stood up to glance around where other men lay in the hushed and yellow roadway. "No more fightin'. I told 'em this is what it'd bring 'em. Let both factions bury their dead now and tend their wounded, and taste the *real* salt — in their tears — and add it up. It wasn't worth it. It never was worth it." He gazed down again. "Doctor; us digger-pine folk would consider it a right fine honour if you'd send us the bill for Deputy Miller. He's a *real* fightin' man, an' in my eyes the only real fightin' men are the ones who fight for what's right an' decent in this life."

Old Withers turned, shouldered through the gathering crowd and led his sombre companions down to where two of their own young men lay dead; down where Grat Younger also lay dead.

It was all over. One man had done it, too, and in doing it had proven to them all that one *good* man can do anything at all, if his heart and soul, and unerring trigger-finger, are co-ordinated with his firmest convictions.

ABOUT THE AUTHOR

Lauran Paine who, under his own name and various pseudonyms has written over 900 books, was born in Duluth, Minnesota, a descendant of the Revolutionary War patriot and author, Thomas Paine. His family moved to California when he was at an early age and his apprenticeship as a Western writer came about through the years he spent in the livestock trade, rodeos, and even motion pictures where he served as an extra because of his expert horsemanship in several films starring movie cowboy Johnny Mack Brown. In the late 1930s, Paine trapped wild horses in Northern Arizona and, for a time, worked as a professional farrier. Paine came to know the Old West through the eyes of many who had been born in the previous century and he learned that Western life had been very different from the way it was portrayed on the screen. "I knew men who had killed other men," he later recalled. "But they were the exceptions. Prior to and during the Depression, people were just too busy eking out an existence to indulge in Saturday-night brawls." He served in the U.S. Navy in the Second World War and began writing for Western pulp magazines following his discharge. It is interesting to note that all of his earliest novels (written under his own name and the pseudonym Mark Carrel) were published in the British market and he soon had as strong a following in that country as in the United States. Paine's Western fiction is characterized by strong plots, authenticity, an apparently effortless ability to construct situation and character, and a preference for building his stories upon a solid foundation of historical fact. *Adobe Empire* (1956), one of his best novels, is a fictionalized account of the last twenty years in the life of trader William Bent and, in an off-trail way, has a melancholy, bittersweet texture that is not easily forgotten. *Moon Prairie* (1950), first published in the United States in 1994, is a memorable story set during the mountain man period of the frontier. In later novels such as *The Homesteaders* (1986) or *The Open Range Men* (1990), he showed that the special magic and power of his stories and characters had only matured along with his basic themes of changing times, changing attitudes, learning from experience, respecting nature, and the yearning for a simpler, more moderate way of life. His most recent Western novels include *Tears of the Heart, Lockwood* and *The White Bird.*

We hope you have enjoyed this Large Print book. Other Thorndike, Wheeler, Kennebec, and Chivers Press Large Print books are available at your library or directly from the publishers.

For information about current and upcoming titles, please call or write, without obligation, to:

Publisher
Thorndike Press
295 Kennedy Memorial Drive
Waterville, ME 04901
Tel. (800) 223-1244

or visit our Web site at:

http://gale.cengage.com/thorndike

OR

Chivers Large Print
published by BBC Audiobooks Ltd
St James House, The Square
Lower Bristol Road
Bath BA2 3SB
England
Tel. +44(0) 800 136919
email: bbcaudiobooks@bbc.co.uk
www.bbcaudiobooks.co.uk

All our Large Print titles are designed for easy reading, and all our books are made to last.